Bronson Howard

Shenandoah

A Military Comedy in Four Acts

Bronson Howard

Shenandoah
A Military Comedy in Four Acts

ISBN/EAN: 9783744787314

Printed in Europe, USA, Canada, Australia, Japan

Cover: Foto ©Andreas Hilbeck / pixelio.de

More available books at **www.hansebooks.com**

SHENANDOAH

A

Military Comedy in Four Acts

BY

BRONSON HOWARD

CAST OF CHARACTERS

GENERAL HAVERILL,
COLONEL KERCHIVAL WEST,
CAPTAIN HEARTSEASE,
FRANK BEDLOE,
} Officers of Sheridan's Cavalry

GENERAL IRANEUS BUCKTHORN, } Commander of the 19th Army Corps.

SERGEANT BARKET.
COLONEL ROBERT ELLINGHAM, 10th Virginian.
CAPTAIN THORNTON, Secret Service C. S. A.
HARDWICK, Surgeon.
CAPTAIN, U. S. SIGNAL CORPS.
CORPORAL DUNN.
BENSON.
LIEUTENANT OF INFANTRY.
MRS. HAVERILL.
GERTRUDE ELLINGHAM.
MADELINE WEST.
JENNY BUCKTHORN, U. S. A.
MRS. EDITH HAVERILL.
OLD MARGERY.
JANNETTE.

COSTUMES.

HAVERILL.—Act 1st. Full Evening Dress.—Acts 2nd and 3rd. Uniform of Brigadier-General, U. S. Vol., 1864. Active Service, rough and war-worn.—Act 4th. Civil Costume. Prince Albert, &c.

KERCHIVAL WEST.—Act 1st. Full Evening Dress.—Acts 2nd and 3rd. Uniform of Colonel of Cavalry, U. S. Vol., 1864 (with cloak in Act 3rd.) Active Service, rough and war-worn.—Act. 4th. Travelling.

CAPT. HEARTSEASE.—Act 2nd. Uniform of Captain of Cavalry, 1864; as neat and precise as is consistent with Active Service.—Act 4th. Afternoon; Civil.

LIEUT. FRANK BEDLOE.—Act 2nd. Lieutenant of Cavalry, 1864; Active Service.—Act 3rd. Same, disarranged for wounded man on stretcher.

GEN. BUCKTHORN.—Acts 2nd and 3rd. Major General, 1864. Active Service.—Act 4th. Citizen; Afternoon.

SERGEANT BARKET.—Acts 2nd and 3rd, Sergeant: Cavalry, U. S. Vol., 1864. Active Service.—Act 4th. Plain undress uniform, sacque or jacket.

ROBERT ELLINGHAM.—Act 1st. Full Evening Dress.—Act 2nd. Confederate Colonel: Infantry, 1864. Active Service. —Act 4th. Citizen; Afternoon. Prince Albert (Grey).

EDWARD THORNTON.—Act 1st. Riding, but not present English cut.—Act 2nd. First, Confederate Captain of Cavalry. Active Service. Second costume, same, in shirt sleeves and without hat or cap.

HARDWICK.—Uniform of Confederate Surgeon, 1864. Active Service.

great

Grant CORPORAL DUNN.—Uniform of rank, Cavalry, U. S. Vol., 1864. Active Service.

The Cava

curately as pr

Signals are also Uniform of 2nd Corporal, Cavalry, U. S. Vol., 1864.

Code. ve Service.

LIEUT. OF INFANTRY.—Uniform of rank, U. S. Vol., 1864. Active Service.

MRS. HAVERILL.—Act 1st. Full evening ball dress.—Act 4th. Mourning, but not too deep.

GERTRUDE ELLINGHAM.—Act 1st. Riding habit.—Act 2d. 1st costume, afternoon at home; simple enough for the South during war. 2nd costume, picturesque and not conventional dress and hat for riding.—Act 3rd. 1st costume of Act 2nd, or similar.—Act 4th. Neat travelling costume.

MADELINE WEST.—Act 1st. Full evening ball dress.—Act 2nd. Pretty afternoon costume.—Act 3rd. Same or walking. —Act 4th. Afternoon costume at home.

JENNY BUCKTHORN.—Act 2nd. Pretty afternoon costume, with military cut trimmings and general air.—Act 3rd. Same. —Act 4th. Afternoon costume at home.

MRS. EDITH HAVERILL. –Young widow's costume.

OLD MARGERY.—Neat old family servant.

JANNETTE.—Young servant.

FOR PROGRAMME.

In ACT I, just before the opening of the war, HAVERILL is a Colonel in the Regular Army. KERCHIVAL WEST and ROBERT ELLINGHAM are Lieutenants in his regiment, having been class-mates at West Point.

ACT I.

CHARLESTON HARBOR IN 1861. AFTER THE BALL.

The citizens of Charleston knew almost the exact hour at which the attack on Fort Sumpter would begin, and they gathered in the gray twilight of the morning to view the bombardment as a spectacle.—*Nicolay, Campaigns of the Civil War, Vol. 1*

" I shall open fire in one hour."—*Beauregard's last message to Major Anderson. Sent at 3.20 A. M., April 12, 1861.*

ACTS II & III.

The Union Army, under General Sheridan, and the Confederate Army, under General Early, were encamped facing each other about twenty miles south of Winchester, on Cedar Creek. * * * Gen. Sheridan was called to Washington. Soon after he left, a startling despatch was taken by our own Signal Officers from the Confederate Signal Station on Three Top Mountain.—*Pond, Camp. Civ. War., Vol. XI.*

On the morning of Oct. 19th, the Union Army was taken completely by surprise. Thoburn's position was swept in an instant. Gordon burst suddenly upon the left flank. The men who escaped capture streamed through the camps along the road to Winchester.—*Pond, supra.*

Far away in the rear was heard cheer after cheer.—*Three years in the Sixth Corps.*

ACT IV.

WASHINGTON, 1865. RESIDENCE OF GENERAL BUCKTHORN.

I feel that we are on the eve of a new era, when there is to be great harmony between the Federal and Confederate.—*Gen. Grant's Memoirs.*

The Cavalry Trumpet Signals in Acts II and III are given accurately as provided in the U. S. Cavalry Tactics. The Torch Signals are also strictly correct, in accordance with the Service Code.

ORCHESTRA MUSIC.

ACT I.

Rise of curtain.—"Dixie."
Fall of curtain.—"When this Cruel War is Over."

ACT II.

Rise of curtain.—Military strain, with suggestion of cavalry trumpet calls, the orchestra to stop as curtain rises, and bugles on the stage continuing.
Fall of curtain.—No music.

ACT III.

Rise of curtain.—Same as at Act II.
Fall of curtain.—"John Brown," beginning at the passage "Glory, Glory, Hallelujah!" Very strong.

ACT IV.

Rise of curtain—Same as fall of Act I.
Fall of curtain.—"Johnnie Comes Marching Home," beginning of the refrain. Sudden and strong.

SHENANDOAH.

ACT I.

CHARLESTON HARBOR IN 1861.   "AFTER THE BALL."

SCENE.—*A Southern Residence on the shore of Charleston Harbor. Interior.—Large double doors up* C., *open. Large, wide window, with low sill, extending down* R. C. *and* R.   *Veranda beyond the doors* C., *and extending down* R. *beyond window. A wide opening up* L. C., *with corridor beyond.* D. *down* L. I. E. *Furniture and appointments quaint and old-fashioned, but an air of brightness and of light; the general tone of the walls and upholstery that of the old Colonial period in its more ornamental and decorative phase, as shown in the early days of Charleston. Old candlesticks and candelabra, with lighted candles nearly burned down.   Beyond the central doors and the window* R. C. *there is a lawn, with southern foliage, extending down to the shores of the harbor; a part of the bay lies in the distance, with low-lying land beyond.   The lights of Charleston are seen over the water along the shore up* C.   *Moonlight. The gray twilight of early morning gradually steals over the scene as the Act progresses.*

DISCOVERED.—*As the curtain rises,* KERCHIVAL WEST *is sitting in a chair,* L. C., *his feet extended and his head thrown back, a handkerchief over his face.* ROBERT ELLINGHAM *strolls in on veranda,* R., *beyond window, smoking.   He looks* R., *starts and moves to window; leans against the upper side of the window and looks across.*

ELLING.   Kerchival!

KERCHIVAL.   (*Under handkerchief.*)   Eh?   H'm!

ELLING.   Can you sleep at a time like this?   My own nerves are on fire

KER.   Fire?   Oh—yes—I remember.   Any more fireworks, Bob?

ELLING.   A signal rocket from one of the batteries, now and then.   (*Goes up beyond window.* KER. *arouses himself, taking handkerchief from his eyes.*)

KER.   What a preposterous hour to be up.   The ball was over an hour ago, all the guests are gone, and it's nearly four o'clock. (*Looks at his watch.*)   Exactly ten minutes of four.   (*Takes out a cigar.*)   Our Southern friends assure us that General Beauregard is to open fire on Fort Sumpter this morning.   I don't believe it. (*Lighting cigar and rising,* X.'s R. C. *and looks out through window.*) There lies the old fort—solemn and grim as ever, and the flag-staff stands above it, like a warning finger.   If they do fire upon it—(*shutting his teeth for a moment and looking down at the cigar in his hand*)—the echo of that first shot will be heard above their graves, and Heaven knows how many of our own, also; but the flag will still float!—over the graves of both sides.

[ELLINGHAM *enters up* C. *and comes down* L. C.]

Are you Southerners all mad, Robert?

ELLING. Are you Northeners all blind? (KERCH. *sits* R. C.) We Virginians would prevent a war if we could. But your people in the North do not believe that one is coming. You do not understand the determined frenzy of my fellow Southerners. Look! (*Pointing up* C.) Do you see the lights of the city, over the water? The inhabitants of Charleston are gathering, even now, in the gray, morning twilight, to witness the long-promised bombardment of Fort Sumpter. It is to be a gala day for them. They have talked and dreamed of nothing else for weeks. The preparations have become a part of their social life—of their amusement—their gayeties. This very night at the ball—here—in the house of my own relatives—what was their talk? What were the jests they laughed at? Sumpter! War! Ladies were betting bonbons that the United States would not dare to fire a shot in return, and pinning ribbons on the breasts of their "heroes." There was a signal rocket from one of the forts, and the young men who were dancing here left their partners standing on the floor to return to the batteries—as if it were the night before another Waterloo. The ladies themselves hurried away to watch the "spectacle" from their own verandas. You won't see the truth! I tell you, Kerchival, a war between the North and South is inevitable!

KER. And if it does come, you Virginians will join the rest.

ELLING. Our State will be the battle ground, I fear. But every loyal son of Virginia will follow her flag. It is our religion!

KER. My State is New York. If New York should go against the old flag, New York might go to the devil. That is my religion!

ELLING. So differently have we been taught what the word "patriotism" means!

KER. You and I are officers in the same regiment of the United States Regular Army, Robert; we were classmates at West Point, and we have fought side by side on the plains. You saved my scalp once; I'd have to wear a wig, now, if you hadn't. I say, old boy, are we to be enemies?

ELLING. (*Laying his hand over his shoulder.*) My dear old comrade, whatever else comes, our friendship shall be unbroken!

KER. Bob! (*Looking up at him.*) I only hope that we shall never meet in battle!

ELLING. In battle? (*Stepping down front.*) The idea is horrible!

KER. (*Rising and crossing to him.*) My dear old comrade, one of us will be wrong in this great fight, but we shall both be honest in it. (*Gives hand,* ELLINGHAM *grasps it warmly, then turns away.*)

ELLING. (*Looking up* R.) Colonel Haverhill is watching the forts, also; he has been as sad to-night as we have. (*X.'s* L.) Next to leaving you, my greatest regret is that I must resign from his regiment.

KER. You are his favorite officer.

ELLING. Naturally, perhaps; he was my guardian. (*Walking down* L.)

[*Enter* HAVERILL *up* C. *He walks down, stopping* C.]

HAVERILL. Kerchival! I secured the necessary passports to the North yesterday afternoon; this one is yours; I brought it down for you early in the evening. (KERCH. *takes paper. Goes to window.*) I am ordered direct to Washington at once, and shall start with Mrs. Haverill this forenoon. You will report to Capt. Lyon, of the 2d Regiment, in St. Louis. Robert! I have hoped for peace to the last, but it is hoping against hope. I feel certain, now, that the fatal blow will be struck this morning. Our old regiment is already broken up, and you, also, will now resign, I suppose, like nearly all your fellow Southerners in the service.

ELLING. You know how sorry I am to leave your command, Colonel!

HAVER. I served under your father in Mexico; he left me, at his death, the guardian of you and your sister Gertrude. Even since you became of age, I have felt that I stood in his place. But you must be your sister's only guardian now. Your father fell in battle, fighting for our common country, but you——

ELLING. He would have done as I shall do, had he lived. He was a Virginian!

HAVER. (*X.* L.) I am glad, Robert, that he was never called upon to decide between two flags. He never knew but one, and we fought under it together. [*Exit* L. 1. E.

ELLING. Kerchival! Something occurred in this house to-night which—which I shouldn't mention under ordinary circumstances, but I—I feel that it may require my further attention, and you, perhaps, can be of service to me. Mrs. Haverill, the wife of the Colonel——

KERCH. Fainted away in her room.

ELLING. You know?

KERCH. I was one of the actors in the little drama.

ELLING. Indeed!

KER. About half-past nine this evening, while the ladies were dressing for the ball, I was going upstairs; I heard a quick, sharp cry, sprang forward, found myself at an open door. Mrs. Haverill lay on the floor inside, as if she had just reached the door to cry for help, when she fell. After doing all the unnecessary and useless things I could think of, I rushed out of the room to tell your sister, Gertrude, and my own sister, Madeline, to go and take care of the lady. Within less than twenty minutes afterwards, I saw Mrs. Haverill sail into the drawing-room, a thing of beauty, and with the glow of perfect health on her cheek. It was an immense relief to me when I saw her. Up to that time 1 had a vague idea that I had committed a murder.

ELLING. Murder!

KER. M—m. A guilty conscience. Every man, of course, does exactly the wrong thing when a woman faints. When I rushed out of Mrs. Haverhill's room, I left my handkerchief soaked with water upon her face. I must ask her for it, it's a silk one. Luckily, the girls got there in time to take it off; she wouldn't have come to if they hadu't. It never occurred to me that she'd need to breathe in my absence. That's all 1 know about the matter. What troubles you? I suppose every woman has a right to faint whenever she chooses. The scream that I heard was so sharp, quick and intense that——

ELLING. That the cause must have been a serious one.

KER. Yes! So I thought. It must have been a mouse.

ELLING. Mr. Edward Thornton has occupied the next room to that of Mrs. Haverhill to night.

KER. (*X. c. quickly.*) What do you mean?

ELLING. During the past month or more, he has been pressing, not to say insolent, in his attentions to Mrs. Haverhill.

KER. I've noticed that myself.

ELLING. (*X. c.*). And he is an utterly unscrupulous man; it is no fault of mine that he was asked to be a guest at this house to-night. He came to Charleston, some years ago, from the North, but if there are any vices and passions peculiarly strong in the South, he has carried them all to the extreme. In one of the many scandals connected with Edward Thornton's name, it was more than was whispered that he entered a lady's room unexpectedly at night. But, as he killed the lady's husband in a duel a few days afterwards, the scandal dropped. (*X. L.*)

KER. Of course; the gentleman received ample satisfaction as an outraged husband, and Mr. Thornton apologized, I suppose, to his widow.

ELLING. He has repeated the adventure.

KER. Do—you—think—that?

ELLING. I was smoking on the lawn, and glanced up at the window; my eyes may have deceived me, and I must move cautiously in the matter; but it couldn't have been imagination; the shadow of Edward Thornton's face and head appeared upon the curtain.

KER. Whew! The devil!

ELLING. Just at that moment I, too, heard the stifled scream.

[*Enter* EDWARD THORNTON, L. 1 E.]

THORNTON. Gentlemen!

ELLING. Your name was just on my tongue, Mr. Thornton.

THORNTON. I thought I heard it, but you are welcome to it. Miss Gertrude has asked me to ride over to Mrs. Pinckney's with her, to learn if there is any further news from the 1 atteries. I am very glad the time to attack Fort Sumpter has come at last!

ELLING. I do not share your pleasure.

THORNTON. You are a Southern gentleman.

ELLING. And you are a Northern "gentleman."

THORNTON. A Southerner by choice; I shall join the cause.

ELLING. We native Southerners will defend our own rights, sir; you may leave them in our keeping. It is my wish, Mr. Thornton, that you do not accompany my sister.

THORNTON. Indeed!

ELLING. Her groom, alone, will be sufficient.

THORNTON As you please, sir. Kindly offer my excuses to Miss Gertrude. You and I can chat over the subject later in the day, when we are alone. (*Moving up stage.*)

ELLING. By all means, and another subject, also, perhaps.

THORNTON. I shall be entirely at your service.

[*Exit* C. *and down* R. *on veranda.*

ELLING. Kerchival, I shall learn the whole truth, if possible, to-day. If it is what I suspect—what I almost know—I will settle with him myself. He has insulted our Colonel's wife and outraged the hospitality of my friends. (*Walking* R.)

KER. (*Walking* L.) By Jove! I think it ought to be my quarrel. I'm sure I'm mixed up in it enough.

MADELINE (*Without, down* L., *calling.*) Kerchival!

ELLING. Madeline! (*Aside, starting,* KERCHIVAL *looks across at him sharply.*)

KER. (*Aside.*) I distinctly saw Bob give a start when he heard Madeline. Now, what can there be about my sister's voice to make a man jump like that?

GERT. (*Without, up* L.) Brother Robert!

KER. Gertrude! (*Aside, starting,* ELLINGHAM *looks at him sharply.*) How the tones of a woman's voice thrill through a man's soul!

[*Enter* MADELINE, L. 1 E.]

MADELINE. Oh, Kerchival—here you are.

[*Enter* GERTRUDE, *up* L. C. *from apartment, in a riding habit, with whip, etc.*]

GERT. Robert, dear! (*Coming down across* C. *to* ROBERT; *they converse in dumb show.*)

MADELINE. Where are your field glasses? I've been rummaging all through your clothes, and swords, and sashes, and things. I've turned everything in your room upside down.

KER. Have you?

MADELINE. I can't find your glasses anywhere. I want to look at the forts. Another rocket went up just now. (*Runs up* C. *and stands on piazza looking off* R)

KER. A sister has all the privileges of a wife to upset a man's things, without her legal obligation to put them straight again. (*Glances at* GERT.) I wish Bob's sister had the same privileges in my room that my own has.

GERT. Mr. Thornton isn't going with me, you say?

ELLING. He requested me to offer you his apologies.

KER. May *I* accompany you? (ELLING. *turns to window* R.)

GERT. My groom, old Pete, will be with me, of course; there's no particular need of anyone else. But you may go along, if you like. I've got my hands full of sugar plums for Jack. Dear old

Jack—he always has his share when we have company. I'm going over to Mrs. Pinckney's to see if she's had any more news from General Beauregard; her son is on the General's staff.

MADELINE (*Looking off* R.) There's another rocket from Fort Johnson; and it is answered from Fort Moultrie. Ah! (*Angrily.*) General Beauregard is a bad, wicked man! (*Coming down.*)

GERT. Oh! Madeline! You are a bad, wicked Northern girl to say such a thing!

MAD. I *am* a Northern girl.

GERT. And I am a Southern girl. (*They face each other.*)

KER. The war has begun. (*Dropping into chair,* L. ELLING. *has turned from window; he strolls across* L., *watching the girls.*)

GERT. General Beauregard is a patriot.

MAD. He is a Rebel!

GERT. So am I.

MAD. Gertrude!—You—you——

GERT. Madeline!—You——

MADELINE. I—I——

GERT. I——

BOTH. O—O–h! (*Bursting into tears and rushing into each other's arms, sobbing, then suddenly kissing each other vigorously.*)

KER. I say, Bob, if the North and South do fight, that will be the end of it

GERT. I've got something to say to you, Madeline, dear. (*Confidentially and turning* R. *with her arms about her waist. The girls sit* R. C. *talking earnestly.*)

ELLING. Kerchival, old boy! There's—there's something I'd like to say to you before we part to-day.

KER. I'd like a word with you, also!

MAD. You don't really mean that, Gertrude—with me?

ELLING. I'm in love with your sister, Madeline.

KER. The devil you are!

ELLING. I never suspected such a thing until last night.

GERT. Robert was in love with you six weeks ago. (MADELINE *kisses her.*)

KER. *I've* made a discovery, too, Bob.

MAD. *I've* got something to say to *you*, Gertrude.

KER. I'm in love with *your* sister.

ELLING. (*Astonished.*) You are?

MAD. Kerchival has been in love with you for the last three months. (GERT. *offers her lips—they kiss*).

KER. I fell in love with her the day before yesterday. (*The two gentlemen grasp each other's hand warmly.*)

ELLING. We understand each other, Kerchival. (*He turns up* C., *stops at door.*) Miss Madeline, you said just now that you wished to watch the forts. Would you like to walk down to the shore?

MADELINE. Yes! (*Rising and going up to him. He takes one of her hands in his own and looks at her earnestly.*)

ELLING. This will be the last day that we shall be together, for the present. But we shall meet again—some time—if we both live.

MAD. If we both live! You mean—if *you* live. You must go into this dreadful war, if it comes.

ELLING. Yes, Madeline, I must. Come let us watch for our fate. [*Exeunt* C. D. *and on veranda* R.

KER. (*Aside.*) I must leave Charleston to-day. (*Sighs.*) Does she love me?

GER. I am ready to start, Mr. West, when you are.

KER. Oh! Of course, I forgot. (*Rising*) I shall be delighted to ride at your side.

GERT. At my side! (*Rising.*) There isn't a horse in America that can keep by the side of my Jack, when I give him his head, and I'm sure to do it. You may follow us. But you can hardly ride in that costume; while you are changing it, I'll give Jack his bonbons. (*Turning to window* R.) There he is, bless him! Pawing the ground, and impatient for me to be on his back. Let him come, Pete. (*Holding up bonbons at window.*) I love you.

KER. Eh? (*Turning suddenly.*)

GERT. (*Looking at him.*) What?

KER. You were saying——

GERT. Jack! (*Looking out. The head of a large black horse appears through the window.*) You dear old fellow! (*Feeds with bonbons*) Jack has been my boy ever since he was a little colt. I brought you up, didn't I, Jack? He's the truest, and kindest, and best of friends; I wouldn't be parted from him for the world, and I'm the only woman he'll allow to be near him.

KER. (*Earnestly.*) You are the only woman, Miss Gertrude, that I——

GERT. Dear Jack!

KER (*Aside.*) Jack embarrasses me. He's a third party.

GERT. There! That will do for the present, Jack. Now go along with Pete! If you are a very good boy, and you don't let Lieutenant Kerchival West come within a quarter of a mile of me, after the first three minutes, you shall have some more sugar plums when we get to Mrs. Pinckney's. (*An old negro leads the horse away.* GERT. *looks around at* KER.) You haven't gone to dress yet; we shall be late. Mrs. Pinckney asked a party of friends to witness the bombardment this morning, and breakfast together on the piazza while they are looking at it. We can remain and join them, if you like.

KER. I hope they won't wait for breakfast until the bombardment begins.

GERT. I'll bet you an embroidered cigar-case, Lieutenant, against a box of gloves that it will begin in less than an hour.

KER. Done! You will lose the bet. But you shall have the gloves; and one of the hands that go inside them shall be—— (*Taking one of her hands; she withdraws it.*)

GERT. My own—until some one wins it You don't believe that General Beauregard will open fire on Fort Sumpter this morning?

KER. No; I don't.

GERT. Everything is ready.

KER. It's so much easier to get everything ready to do a thing than it is to do it. I have been ready a dozen times, this very night, to say to you, Miss Gertrude, that I—that I——(*Pauses.*)

GERT. (*Looking down and tapping skirt with her whip.*) Well?

KER. But I didn't.

GERT. (*Glancing up at him suddenly.*) I dare say, General Beauregard has more nerve than you have.

KER. It is easy enough to set the batteries around Charleston Harbor, but the man who fires the first shot at a woman——

GERT. Woman!

KER. At the American flag—must have nerves of steel.

GERT. You Northern men are so slow, to——

KER. I have been slow; but I assure you, Miss Gertrude, that my heart——

GERT. What subject are we on now?

KER. You were complaining because I was too slow.

GERT. I was doing nothing of the kind, sir!—let me finish, please. You Northern men are so slow, to believe that our Southern heroes—Northern *men* and Southern *heroes*—you recognize the distinction I make—you won't believe that they will keep their promises. They have sworn to attack Fort Sumpter this morning, and—they—will do it. This "American Flag" you talk of is no longer our flag ; it is foreign to us !—It is the flag of an enemy !

KER. (*Tenderly and earnestly.*) Am I your enemy?

GERT. You have told me that you will return to the North, and take the field.

KER. Yes, I will. (*Decisively.*)

GERT. You will be fighting against my friends, against my own brother, against me. We *shall* be enemies.

KER. (*Firmly.*) Even that, Gertrude—(*She looks around at him, he looks squarely into her eyes as he proceeds*)—if you will have it so. If my country needs my services, I shall not refuse them, though it makes us enemies ! (*She wavers a moment, under strong emotion, and turns away; sinks upon the seat L., her elbow on the back of it, and her tightly-clenched fist against her cheek, looking away from him.*)

GERT. I will have it so ! I am a Southern woman !

KER. We have more at stake between us, this morning, than a cigar case and a box of gloves. (*Turning up stage.*)

(*Enter MRS. HAVERHILL up L. C., from apartment.*)

MRS. H. Mr. West! I've been looking for you. I have a favor to ask.

KER. Of me?—with pleasure.

MRS. H. But I am sorry to have interrupted you and Gertrude. (*Passing down R., KER. moves up C., GERT. rises.*) (*Apart.*) There are tears in your eyes, Gertrude, dear !

GERT. (*Apart*) They have no right there.

MRS. H. (*Apart.*) I'm afraid I know what has happened. A quarrel ! and you are to part with each other so soon. Do not let a girl's coquetry trifle with her heart until it is too late. You remember the confession you made to me last night ?

GERT. (*Apart.*) Constance! (*Starting.*) That is my secret; more a secret now than ever.

MRS. H. (*Apart.*) Yes, dear; but you do love him. (GER-TRUDE *moves up* C.)

GERT. You need not ride over with me, Mr. West.

KER. I can be ready in one moment.

GERT. I choose to go alone! Old Pete will be with me; and Jack, himself, is a charming companion.

KER. If you prefer Jack's company to mine——

GERT. I do. [*Exit* C. *on veranda and down* R.

KER. Damn Jack! But you will let me assist you to mount.
[*Exit after her.*

MRS. H. We leave for the North before noon, but every hour seems a month. If my husband should learn what happened in my room to night, he would kill that man. What encouragement could I have given him? Innocence is never on its guard—but, (*Drawing up.*) the last I remember before I fell unconscious, he was crouching before me like a whipped cur! (*Starts as she looks out of the window.*) There is Mr. Thornton, now —Ah! (*Angrily.*) No—I must control my own indignation. I must keep him and Colonel Haverill from meeting before we leave Charleston. Edward Thornton would shoot my husband down without remorse. But poor Frank! I must not forget him, in my own trouble. I have but little time left to care for his wellfare.

[*Re-enter* KERCHIVAL, C.]

KER. You said I could do you a favor, Mrs. Haverill?

MRS. H. Yes, I wanted to speak with you about General Haverill's son, Frank. I should like you to carry a message to Charleston for me, as soon as it is light. It is a sad errand. You know too well the great misfortune that has fallen upon my husband in New York.

KER. His only son has brought disgrace upon his family name, and tarnished the reputation of a proud soldier. Colonel Haverill's fellow officers sympathize with him most deeply.

MRS. H. And poor young Frank! I could hardly have loved the boy more if he had been my own son. If he had not himself confessed the crime against the bank, I could not have believed him guilty. He has escaped from arrest. He is in the City of Charleston. I am the only one in all the world he could turn to. He was only a lad of fourteen when his father and I were married, six years ago; and the boy has loved me from the first. His father is stern and bitter now in his humiliation. This note from Frank was handed to me while the company were here last evening. I want you to find him and arrange for me to meet him, if you can do it with safety. I shall give you a letter for him.

KER. I'll get ready at once; and I will do all I can for the boy. (*Turning up* L. C.)

MRS. H. And—Mr. West! Gertrude and Madeline have told me that—that—I was under obligations to you last evening.

KER. Don't mention it. I merely ran for them, and I—I'm very glad you didn't choke—before they reached you. I trust you are quite well now?

MRS. H. I am entirely recovered, thank you. And I will ask another favor of you, for we are old friends. I desire very much that General Haverill should not know that—that any accident occurred to me to-night—or that my health has not been perfect.

KER. Certainly, madam!

MRS. H. It would render him anxious without cause.

KER. (*Aside.*) It looks as if Robert was right: she doesn't want the two men to meet.

[*Enter* HAVERILL, L. C. A *white silk handkerchief in his hand.*]

t HAVER. Constance, my dear, I've been all over the place looking for you. I thought you were in your room. But—by the way, Kerchival, this is your handkerchief; your initials are on it. (KERCHIVAL *turns and stares at him a second.* MRS. HAVERILL *starts slightly and turns front.* HAVER. *glances quickly from one to the other, then extends his hands toward* KERCHIVAL, *with the handkerchief.* KER. *moves to him and takes it.* MRS. HAVER. *drops into chair,* R. C.)

KER. Thank you. (*He walks up and exits* L. C., *with a quick glance back.* HAVER. *looks at* MRS. HAVERILL, *who sits nervously, looking away. He then glances up* L. C. *after* KER. *A cloud comes over his face and he stands a second in thought. Then, with a movement as if brushing away a passing suspicion, he smiles pleasantly and approaches* MRS. H.; *leans over her.*)

HAVER. My fair Desdemona! (*Smiling.*) I found Cassio's handkerchief in your room. Have you a kiss for me? (*She looks up, he raises her chin with a finger and kisses her.*) That's the way I shall smother you.

MRS. H. (*Rising and dropping her head upon his breast.*) Husband!

HAVER. But what is this they have been telling me?

MRS. H. What have they said to you?

HAVER. There was something wrong with you in the early part of the evening; you are trembling and excited, my girl!

MRS. H. It was nothing, John; I—I—was ill, for a few moments, but I am well now.

HAVER. You said nothing about it to me.

MRS. H. Do not give it another thought.

HAVER. Was there anything besides your health involved in the affair? There was. (*Aside.*) How came this handkerchief in her room?

MRS. H My husband! I do not want to say anything more—at—at present—about what happened to-night. There has never been a shadow between us—will you not trust me?

HAVER. Shadow! You stand in a bright light of your own, my wife; it shines upon my whole life—there can be no shadow there. Tell me as much or as little as you like, and in your own time. I am sure you will conceal nothing from me that I ought to know. I trust my honor and my happiness to you, absolutely.

MRS. H. They will both be safe, John, in my keeping. But

there is something else that I wish to speak with you about; something very near to your heart—your son!

HAVER. My son!

MRS. H. He is in Charleston.

HAVER. And not—in prison? To me he is nowhere. I am childless.

MRS. H. I hope to see him to-day; may I not take him some kind word from you?

HAVER. My lawyers in New York had instructions to provide him with whatever he needed.

MRS. H. They have done so, and he wants for nothing; he asks for nothing except that I will seek out the poor young wife—only a girl herself—whom he is obliged to desert, in New York.

HAVER. His marriage was a piece of reckless folly, but I forgave him that.

MRS. H. I am sure that it was only after another was dependent on him that the debts of a mere spendthrift were changed to fraud—and crime.

HAVER. You may tell him that I will provide for her.

MRS. H. And may I take him no warmer message from his father?

HAVER. I am an officer of the United States Army. The name which my son bears came to me from men who had borne it with honor, and I transmitted it to him without a blot. He has disgraced it, by his own confession.

MRS. H. I cannot forget the poor mother who died when he was born; her whose place I have tried to fill, to both Frank and to you. I never saw her, and she is sleeping in the old graveyard at home. But I am doing what she would do to-day, if she were living. No pride—no disgrace—could have turned her face from him. The care and the love of her son has been to me the most sacred duty which one woman can assume for another.

HAVER. You have fulfilled that duty, Constance. Go to my son! I would go with you, but he is a man now; he could not look into my eyes, and I could not trust myself. But I will send him something which a man will understand. Frank loves you as if you were his own mother; and I—I would like him to—to think tenderly of me, also. He will do it when he looks at this picture. (*Taking a miniature from his pocket.*)

MRS. H. Of me?

HAVER. I have never been without it one hour, before, since we were married. He will recognize it as the one that I have carried through every campaign, in every scene of danger on the Plains; the one that has always been with me. He is a fugitive from justice. At times, when despair might overcome him, this may give him nerve to meet his future life manfully. It has often nerved me, when I might have failed without it. Give it to him, and tell him that I send it. (*Giving her the miniature.*) I could not send a kinder message, and he will understand it. (*Turning L., stands a moment in thought. THORNTON appears at window R., looking at them quietly, over his shoulder, a cigar in his hand.*

MRS. H. *sees him and starts with a suppressed breath, then looks at* HAVER., *who moves* L. *Aside.*) My son! My son! We shall never meet again! [*Exit* L. 1 E., *in thought.*

(MRS. H. *looks after him earnestly, then turns and looks at* THORNTON, *drawing up to her full height.* THORNTON *moves up stage, beyond window.*)

MRS. H. (*Moving* R. *front.*) Will he dare to speak to me again? (*Enter* THORNTON *up* C.; *he comes down* L. C., *quietly. He has thrown away cigar.*)

THORN. Mrs. Haverill! I wish to offer you an apology!

MRS. H. I have not asked for one, sir !   •

THORN. Do you mean by that, that you will not accept one ?

MRS. H. (*Aside.*) What can I say? (*Aloud.*) Oh, Mr. Thornton!—for my husband's sake, I——

THORN. Ah ! You are afraid that your husband may become involved in an unpleasant affair. Your solicitude for his safety, madame, makes me feel that my offence to-night was indeed unpardonable. No gentleman can excuse himself for making such a mistake as I have made. I had supposed that it was Lieutenant Kerchival West who——

MRS. H. What do you mean, sir ?

THORN. But if it is your husband that stands between us——

MRS. H. Let me say this, sir ; whatever I may fear for my husband, he fears nothing for himself.

THORN. He knows? (*Looking at her, keenly.*)

[*Enter* KERCHIVAL WEST, *now in riding suit, up* L. C.]

(*He stops, looking at them.*) You are silent. Your husband does know what occurred to night; that relieves my conscience. (*Lightly.*) Colonel Haverill and I can now settle it between us.

MRS. H. No, Mr. Thornton ! My husband knows nothing, and, I beg of you, do not let this horrible affair go further. (*Sees* KER.)

KER. Pardon me. (*Stepping forward,* C.) I hope I am not interrupting you. (*Aside.*) It *was* Thornton. (*X.* R. C. *Aloud.*) You said you would have a letter for me to carry, Mrs. Haverill.

MRS. H. Yes, I—I will go up and write it at once. (*X. up* L.; *stops and looks back. Aside.*) I wonder how much he overheard.

KER. (*Quietly.*) I suppose eight o'clock will be time enough for me to go ?

MRS. H. Oh, yes! (*glancing at him a moment*)—quite.

[*Exit up* L. C., *through apartment.*

KER. (*Quietly.*) Mr. Thornton ! you are a scoundrel ! Do I make myself plain ?

THORN. You make the fact that you desire to pick a quarrel with me quite plain, sir ; but I choose my own quarrels and my own enemies.

KER. Colonel Haverill is my commander, and he is beloved by every officer in the regiment.

THORNTON. On what authority, may I ask, do you——

KER. The honor of Colonel Haverill's wife is under our protection.

THORNTON. Under your protection? You have a better claim than that, perhaps, to act as her champion. Lieutenant Kerchival West is Mrs. Haverill's favorite officer in the regiment.

KER. (*Approaching him.*) You dare to suggest that I——

THORN. If I accept your challenge, I shall do so not because you are her protector, but my rival.

KER. Bah! (*Striking him sharply on the cheek with glove. The two men stand facing each other a moment.*) Is it my quarrel now?

THORN. I think you are entitled to my attention, sir.

KER. My time here is limited.

THORNTON. We need not delay. The Bayou La Forge is convenient to this place.

KER. I'll meet you there, with a friend, at once.

THORN. It will be light enough to see the sights of our weapons in about one hour. (*They bow to each other, and* THORN. *goes out,* L 1 E.)

KER. I've got ahead of Bob.

GERT. (*Without,* R.) Whoa! Jack! Old boy! Steady, now—that's a good fellow.

KER. She has returned. I *must* know whether Gertrude Ellingham loves me—before Thornton and I meet. He is a good shot.

GERT. (*Without, calling.*) O—h! Pete! You may take Jack to the stable. Ha—ha—ha! (*Appears at window: to* KER.) Old Pete, on the bay horse, has been doing his best to keep up with us; but Jack and I had led him such a race! Ha—ha—ha—ha! (*Disappearing beyond window.*)

KER. Does she love me?

GERT. (*Entering up* C. *and coming down.*) I have the very latest news from the headquarters of the Confederate Army in South Carolina. At twenty minutes after three this morning General Beauregard sent this message to Major Anderson in Fort Sumpter: " I shall open fire in one hour ! " The time is up !—and he will keep his word ! (*Turning* R. *and looking out of the window.* KER. *moves across to her.*)

KER. Gertrude! I must speak to you; we may never meet again; but I must know the truth. I love you. (*Seizing her hand.*) Do you love me? (*She looks around at him as if about to speak ; hesitates.*) Answer me ! (*She looks down with a coquettish smile, tapping her skirt with her riding whip.*) Well? (*A distant report of a cannon, and low rumbling reverberations over the harbor.* GERT. *turns suddenly, looking out* R. KER. *draws up, also looking off.*)

GERT. A low—bright—line of fire--in the sky ! It is a shell. (*A second's pause ; she starts slightly.*) It has burst upon the fort. (*Looks over her shoulder at* KER., *drawing up to her full height.*) Now !—do you believe that we Southerners are in deadly earnest ?

KER. We Northerners are in deadly earnest, too. I have received my answer. (*N.'s quickly, turns.*) We are—enemies ! (*They look at each other for a moment.*)

[*Exit* KERCHIVAL, L. 1 E.

GERT. Kerchival! (*Moving quickly half across stage, looking after him eagerly; stops.*) Enemies! (*She drops into chair* R. C., *sobbing bitterly. Another distant report, and low, long reverberations as the curtain descends.*)

CURTAIN.

ACT II.

SCENE.—*The Ellingham Homestead in the Shenandoah Valley.*
Exterior. Three Top Mountain in the distance. A corner of
the house L. 1 E., with projecting end of veranda. Low wall
extending up from veranda to C. at about 3, then down and out
R. 1 E. A wide opening in the wall from C. to L. C., with a
low, heavy stone post, with flat top, on each side. Beyond the
wall and opening, a road runs across stage, from L. 2 to R.
4 E. At the back of this road, elevation of rock and turf.
This slopes up from out L. 4 E., behind wood wing. It is level
on the top about twelve feet; slopes down to road R. C., and
also out behind wood wings at R. 4 E. The level part in the
centre rises to about four feet above the stage. Beyond this
elevation the distance is a broad valley, with Three Top Moun-
tain rising on the R. C. and R. Foliage appropiate to Northern
Virginia—walnut, cottonwood, etc. Rustic seats and table R. C.
Seat L. C. near veranda. A low rock near the stone post C.
Sunset when curtain rises. As the act proceeds this fades into
twilight and then bright moonlight. The number references for
the trumpet signals, in this and the next act, are to the official
book, entitled "Cavalry Tactics, United States Army," pub-
lished by D. Appleton & Co., N. Y., 1887. The number refer-
ences for the Torch Signals, in this act, are to the General
Service Code. This code may be found, with illustrations and
instructions, in a book entitled "Signal Tactics," by Lieut.
Hugh T. Reed, U. S. Army; published by John Riley and Sons,
10 Astor Place, N. Y., 1880. At rise of curtain, Trumpet
Signal No. 34 or No. 35 is heard, very distant, up L. GER-
TRUDE and MADELINE discovered on elevation up C. GER-
TRUDE is shading her eyes with her hand and looking off L.
MADELINE stands a little below her, on the incline, resting her
arm about GERTRUDE'S waist, also looking off.

GERT. It is a regiment of Union Cavalry. The Federal troops
now have their lines three miles beyond us, and only a month ago
the Confederate Army was North of Winchester. One army or
the other has been marching up and down the Shenandoah Valley
for three years. I wonder what the next change will be. We in
Virginia have had more than our share of the war. (*Looking
off.*)

MAD. You have indeed, Gertrude. (*Walking down L. to seat.*)
And we at home in Washington have pitied you so much. But
everybody says that there will be peace in the valley after this.
(*Dropping into seat, L. C.*)

GERT. Peace! (*Coming down.*) That word means something
very different to us poor Southerns from what it means to you.

MAD. I know, dear; and we in the North know how you have suffered, too. We were very glad when General Buckthorn was appointed to the command of the Nineteenth Army Corps, so that Jenny could get permission for herself and me to come and visit you.

GERT. The old General will do anything for Jenny, I suppose.

MAD. Yes. (*Laughing.*) We say in Washington that Jenny is in command of the Nineteenth Army Corps herself.

GERT. I was never more astonished or delighted in my life than when you and Jenny Buckthorn rode up, this morning, with a guard from Winchester; and Madeline, dear, I—I only wish that my brother Robert could be here, too. Do you remember in Charleston, darling—that morning—when I told you that—that Robert loved you?

MAD. He—(*looking down*)—he told me so himself only a little while afterwards, and while we were standing there, on the shore of the bay—the—the shot was fired which compelled him to enter this awful war—and me to return to my home in the North.

GERT. I was watching for that shot, too. (*Turning L.*)

MAD. Yes—(*rising*)—you and brother, Kerchival——

GERT. We won't talk about that, my dear. We were speaking of Robert. As I told you this morning, I have not heard from him since the battle of Winchester, a month ago. Oh, Madeline! the many, many long weeks, like these, we have suffered, after some terrible battle in which he has been engaged. I do not know, now, whether he is living or dead.

MAD. The whole war has been one long suspense to me. (*Dropping her face into her hands.*)

GERT. My dear sister! (*Placing her arm about her waist and moving L.*) You are a Northern girl, and I am a Rebel—but we are sisters. (*They go up veranda and out L. 2 E.*) *An old country-man comes in on a cane, L. 3 E. He stops R. C. and glances back, raises a broken portion of the capstone of post, R. C., and places a letter under it. GERT. has stepped back on veranda and is watching him. He raises his head sharply, looking at her and bringing his finger to his lips. He drops his head again, as with age, and goes out R. 2 E. GERT. moves down to stage and up to road, looks R. and L., raises the broken stone, glancing back as she does so ; takes letter and moves down.*) Robert is alive ! It is his hand-writing ! (*Tears open the wrapper.*) Only a line from him ! and this—a dispatch—and also a letter to me ! Why, it is from Mrs. Haverill—from Washington—with a United States postmark. (*Reads from a scrap of paper.*)

"The enclosed dispatch must be in the hands of Captain Edward Thornton before eight o'clock to-night. We have signaled to him from Three Top Mountain, and he is waiting for it at the bend in Oak Run. Our trusty scout at the Old Forge will carry it if you will put it in his hands."

The scout is not there, now ; I will carry it to Captain Thornton myself. I—I haven't my own dear horse to depend on now ; Jack knew every foot of the way through the woods about here ; he could have carried a dispatch himself. I can't bear to think of Jack ; it's two years since he was captured by the enemy—and if he is still living—I—I suppose he is carrying one of their officers. No! Jack wouldn't fight on that side. He was a Rebel—as I am. He was one of the Black Horse Cavalry—his eyes always flashed towards the North. Poor Jack! my pet. (*Brushing her eyes*) But this is no time for tears. I must do the best I can with the gray horse. Captain Thornton shall have the dispatch. (*Reads from note.*)

"I also inclose a letter for you. I found it in a United States mail-bag which we captured from the enemy."

Oh—that's the way Mrs. Haverill's letter came—Ha—ha—ha, —by way of the Rebel army ! (*Opens it ; reads.*)

"My Darling Gertrude : When Colonel Kerchival West was in Washington last week, on his way from Chattanooga, to serve under Sheridan in the Shenandoah Valley, he called upon me. It was the first time I had seen him since the opening of the war. I am certain that he still loves you, dear." (*She kisses the letter eagerly, then draws up.*) It is quite immaterial to me whether Kerchival West still loves me or not. (*Reads.*)

" I have kept your secret, my darling."—Ah! My secret !— " but I was sorely tempted to betray the confidence you reposed in me at Charleston. If Kerchival West had heard you say, as I did, when your face was hidden in my bosom, that night, that you loved him with your whole heart——"—Oh ! I could bite my tongue out now for making that confession—(*Looks down at letter with a smile.*) "I am certain that he still loves you." (*Trumpet Signal No. 41. Kisses the letter repeatedly. Trumpet Signal No. 41, louder than at first. She starts, listening.*)

JENNY BUCKTHORN *runs in*, L. 2 E , *on the veranda*.

JEN. Do you hear, Gertrude, they are going to pass this very house. (*Military band. "John Brown" playing in the distance. Chorus of Soldiers.*) I've been watching them through my glass ; it is Colonel Kerchival West's regiment.

GERT. (*Eagerly, then coldly.*) Colonel West's ! It is perfectly indifferent to me whose regiment it is.

JEN. Oh ! Of course. (*Coming down.*) It is equally indifferent to me ; Captain Heartsease is in command of the first troop. (*Trumpet Signal No. 52.*) Column right ! (*She runs up to road C. Looks L.) They are coming up the hill.*

GERT. At my very door! And Kerchival West in command ! I will not stand here and see them pass. (*X. -ing L.*) The despatch for Captain Thornton. I will carry it to him as soon as they are gone. (*Exit up veranda and up L. 2 E., the band and chorus increasing in volume.*)

JEN. Cavalry! That's the branch of the service I was born in ; I was in a fort at the time—on the Plains. Sergeant Barket always said that my first baby squall was a command to the garrison ; if any officer or soldier, from my father down, failed to obey my orders, I court-martialed him on the spot. I'll make 'em pass in review. (*Jumping up on the rustic seat, R. C.*) Yes! (*Looking off L.*) There's Captain Heartsease himself, at the head of the first troop. Draw Sabre! (*With parasol.*) Present! (*Imitating*

*the action. Music. The band and chorus now full and loud; she
swings parasol in time. Trumpet Signal No. 40. Band and
chorus suddenly cease.)* Halt! Why, they are stopping here.
(Trumpet Signal No. 38.) Dismount! I—I wonder if they are
going to—I do believe—*(Looking L. eagerly. Trumpet Signal No.
17.)* Assembly of Guard Details! As sure as fate, they are going
into camp here. We girls will have a jolly time. *(Jumping
down.)* Ha—ha—ha—ha! Let me see. How shall I receive
Captain Heartsease? He deserves a court-martial, for he stole my
lace handerchief—at Mrs. Grayson's reception—in Washington.
He was called away by orders to the West that very night, and
we haven't met since. *(Sighs.)* He's been in lots of battles since
then; I suppose he's forgotten all about the handkerchief. We
girls, at home, don't forget such things. We aren't in battles.
All we can do is to—to scrape lint and flirt with other officers.
(Down R.)

[*Enter* CAPTAIN HEARTSEASE, L. 3 E., *followed by* COLONEL
        ROBERT ELLINGHAM; *stops at gate, L.*]

HEART.   This way, Colonel Eillingham. *(They enter. As
they come down C.* HEARTSEASE *stops suddenly, looking at* JENNY;
puts up his glasses.) Miss Buckthorn!

JEN.   Captain Heartsease!

HEART.   *(Very quietly and with perfect composure.)* I am thun-
der struck. The unexpected sight of you has thrown me into a
fever of excitement.

JEN.   Has it? *(Aside.)* If he gets so excited as that in battle it
must be awful. *(Aloud.)* Colonel Ellingham! *(X.-ing to him;*
HEARTSEASE *walks R.)*

ELLING.   Miss Buckthorn! You are visiting my sister? I am
what may be called a visitor—by force—myself.

JEN.   Oh! You're a prisioner!

ELLING.   I ventured too far within the Union lines to-night,
and they have picked me up. But Major Wilson has kindly ac-
cepted my parole, and I shall make the best of it.

JEN.   Is Major Wilson in command of the regiment?

HEART.   Yes. Colonel West is to join us at this point, during
the evening.

ELLING.   I am very glad you are here, Miss Buckthorn, with
Gertrude.

JEN.   Somebody here will be delighted to see you, Colonel.

ELLING.   My sister can hardly be pleased to see me as a prisoner.

JEN.   Not your sister. *(Passing him and X.-ing to veranda, L.,
turns and beckons to him. She motions with her thumb, over her
shoulder. He goes up the steps of the veranda and turns.)*

ELLING.   What do you mean?

JEN.   I mean this—*(Reaching up her face, he leans down,
placing his ear near her lips.)*—somebody else's sister ! When she
first sees you, be near enough to catch her.

ELLING.   I understand you! Madeline! *(Exit L. 2 E. on
veranda. JENNY runs up steps after him, stops and looks back at
HEARTSEASE over the railing. HEARTSEASE takes a lace hand-*

kerchief from his pocket.)

JEN. I do believe that's my handkerchief. (*A guard of Sentries marches in* L. 3 E. *and across stage in road. The Corporal in command orders halt and a Sentry to post, then marches guard out,* R. 3 E. *The Sentry stands with his back to audience,* R., *afterwards moving out and in* R., *appearing and disappearing during act.*)

HEART. Miss Buckthorn! I owe you an apology. After I left your side, the last time we met, I found your handkerchief in my possession. I assure you, it was an accident. (*Walking* L.)

JEN. (*Aside, pouting*). I thought he *intended* to steal it. (*Aloud.*) That was more than a year ago. (*Then brightly.*) Do you always carry it with you?

HEART. Always; there. (*Indicating his left breast pocket.*)

JEN. Next to his heart!

HEART. Shall I return it to you?

JEN. Oh, if a lace handkerchief can be of any use to you, Captain, during the hardships of a campaign—you—you may keep that one. You soldiers have so few comforts—and it's real lace.

HEART. Thank you. (*Returning handkerchief to his pocket.*) Miss Buckthorn, your papa is in command of the Nineteenth Army Corps. He doesn't like me.

JEN. I know it.

HEART. But you are in command of him.

JEN. Yes; I always have been.

HEART. If ever you decide to assume command of any other man, I—I trust you will give *me* your orders.

JEN. (*Aside, starting back.*) If that was intended for a proposal, it's the queerest-shaped one I ever heard of. (*Aloud.*) Do you mean, Captain, that—that you—— I must command myself now. (*Shouldering her parasol.*) 'Bout—face! March! (*Turning squarely around, marching up and out,* L. 2 E., *on veranda.*)

HEART. I have been placed on waiting orders. (*Stepping up* L. C. *and looking after her; then very quietly and without emotion.*) I am in an agony of suspense. The sight of that girl always arouses the strongest emotions of my nature. (*Enter* COLONEL KERCHIVAL WEST, L. 3 E., *looking at paper in his hand. The Sentinel,* R., *in road, comes to a salute.*) Colonel West!

KER. Captain!

HEART. You have rejoined the regiment sooner than we expected.

KER. (*Looking at paper.*) Yes; General Haverill is to meet me here at seven o'clock. Major Wilson tells me that some of your company captured Colonel Robert Ellingham, of the Tenth Virginia.

HEART. He is here under parole.

KER. And this is the old Ellingham homestead. (*Aside, walking down* R.) Gertrude herself is here, I suppose; almost a prisoner to me, like her brother; and my troops surround their home. She must, indeed, feel that I am her enemy now. Ah,

well, war is war. (*Aloud.*) By the bye, Heartsease, a young
Lieutenant, Frank Bedloe, has joined our troop?

HEART. Yes; an excellent young officer.

KER. I sent for him as I came through the camp. Lieutenant
Frank "Bedloe" is the son of General Haverill.

HEART. Indeed! Under an assumed name!

KER. He was supposed to have been killed in New Orleans
more than a year ago; but he was taken prisoner instead. (*Looking R.*) I should never have known him.

[*Enter* LIEUTENANT FRANK BEDLOE, L. 3 E.; *he stops,* R. C.,
saluting.]

FRANK. You wished me to report to you, Colonel?

KER. You have been assigned to the regiment during my absence.

FRANK. Yes, sir. (KERCHIVAL *moves to him and grasps his
hand; looks into his eyes a moment before speaking.*)

KER. Frank Haverill.

FRANK. You—you know me, sir?

KER. I saw Mrs. Haverill while I was passing through Washington on Saturday. She told me that you had escaped from
prison in Richmond, and had re-entered the service. She did not
know then that you had been assigned to my regiment. I received a letter from her, in Winchester, this morning, informing
me of the fact, and asking for my good offices in your behalf.
But here is the letter. (*Taking letter from wallet and giving it to
him.*) It is for you rather than for me. I shall do everything I
can for you, my dear fellow. (*Walking across, down L.*)

FRANK. Thank you, sir. (*Opens letter, dropping the envelope
upon the table,* R. C.) Kind, thoughtful and gentle to my faults,
as ever—(*Looking at the letter.*)—and always thinking of my
welfare. My poor little wife, too, is under her protection.
Gentlemen, I beg of you not to reveal my secret to my father.

KER. General Haverill shall know nothing from us, my boy,
you have my word for that.

HEART. Nothing.

KER. And he cannot possibly recognize you. What with
your full beard, and thinking as he does, that you are——

FRANK. That I am dead. I am dead to him. It would have
been better if I had died. Nothing but my death—not even
that—can wipe out the disgrace which I brought upon his name.

HEART. Gen. Haverill has arrived. (*Looking* R.)

[*Enter* GENERAL HAVERILL, R. 2 E., *with a Staff Officer.*]

FRANK. (*Moving down* R.) My father!

HAVER. (*Exchanging salutes with the three officers. He turns
to the Staff Officer, giving him a paper and brief instructions in
dumb show, pointing up* R. *The Officer goes out over the incline,*
R. 3 E. *Another Staff Officer enters,* L. 3 E., *salutes and hands him
a paper, then stands up,* L. C.) Ah! The men are ready. (*Looking at the paper, then to* KERCHIVAL.) Colonel! I have a very
important matter to arrange with you; there is not a moment to
be lost. I will ask Captain Heartsease to remain. (FRANK *sa-*

lutes and starts up stage; HAVERILL *looks at him, starting slightly; raises his hand to detain him.*) One moment; your name!

~~HART.~~ Lieutenant Bedloe, General, of my own troop, and one of our best officers. (HAVERILL *steps to* FRANK, *looking into his face a moment.*)

HAVER. Pardon me! (*Stepping down* R. C. FRANK *moves up C., stops and looks back at him.* HAVERILL *stands up a moment in thought, covers his face with one hand, then draws up.*) Colonel West! We have a most dangerous piece of work for a young officer—(FRANK *starts joyfully.*)—to lead a party of men, whom I have already selected. I cannot *order* an officer to undertake anything so nearly hopeless; he must be a volunteer.

FRANK. Oh, sir, General! Let me be their leader.

HAVER. I thought you had passed on.

FRANK. Do not refuse me, sir. (HAVERILL *looks at him a moment.* HEARTSEASE *and* KERCHIVAL *exchange glances.*)

HAVER. You are the man we need, my young friend. You shall go. Listen! We wish to secure a key to the cipher despatches, which the enemy are now sending from their signal station on Three Top Mountain. There is another Confederate Signal Station in the valley, just beyond Buckton's Ford (*Pointing up* L.) Your duty will be this: First, to get inside the enemy's line; then to follow a path through the woods, with one of our scouts as your guide; attack the Station suddenly, and secure their code, if possible. I have this moment received word that the scout and the men are at the fort, now, awaiting their leader. Major McCandless, of my staff, will take you to the place. (*Indicating the Staff Officer.* FRANK *exchanges salutes with him.*) My young friend! I do not conceal from you the dangerous nature of the work on which I am sending you. If—if you do not return, I—I will write, myself, to your friends. (*Taking out note book.*) Have you a father living?

FRANK. My—father—is—is—he is——

HAVERILL. I understand you. A mother? Or——

KER. I have the address of Lieut. Bedloe's friends, General.

HAV. I will ask you to give it to me, if necessary. (*Extends his hand.*) Good-bye, my lad. (FRANK *moves to him.* HAVER. *grasps his hand, warmly.*) Keep a brave heart and come back to us. (FRANK *moves up* C. *Exit Staff Officers.*)

FRANK. He is my father still. [*Exit* L. 2 E.

HAVER. My dead boy's face! (*Dropping his face into both hands.*)

HEART. (*Apart to* KERCHIVAL.) He shall not go alone. (*Aloud.*) General! Will you kindly give me leave of absence from the command?

HAV. Leave of absence! To an officer in active service—and in the presence of the enemy? (*Walking* R.)

KER. (*Taking his hand. Apart.*) God bless you, old fellow! Look after the boy.

HAV. A—h—(*With a sudden thought, turns.*) I think I understand you, Captain Heartsease. Yes; you may have leave of absence.

HEART. Thank you. (*Salutes.* HAVER. *and* KER. *salute.*)

[*Exit* HEART., L. 3 E.

KER. (L.) Have you any further orders for me, General?

HAVER. I wish you to understand the great importance of the duty to which I have just assigned this young officer. General Sheridan started for Washington this noon, by way of Front Royal. Since his departure, we have had reason to believe that the enemy are about to move, and we must be able to read their signal despatches, if possible. (*Sitting*, R. C.) I have ordered Capt. Lockwood, of our own Signal Corps, to report to you here, with officers and men. (*Takes up the empty envelope on table, unconsciously, as he speaks, tapping it on the table.*) If Lieut. Bedloe succeeds in getting the key to the enemy's cipher, we can signal from this point—(*pointing to elevation*)—to our station at Front Royal. Men and horses are waiting there now, to carry forward a message, if necessary, to Gen. Sheridan himself. (*He starts suddenly, looking at the envelope in his hand; reads address. Aside.*) "Colonel Kerchival West"—in my wife's handwriting!

WEST. I'll attend to your orders.

HAVERILL. —Postmarked at Washington, yesterday. (*Reads.*) "Private and confidential." (*Aloud.*) Col. West! I found a paragraph, to-day, in a paper published in Richmond, taken from a prisoner. I will read it to you. (*Takes newspaper slip from his wallet and reads.*)

"From the Charleston Mercury. Captain Edward Thornton, of the Confederate Secret Service, has been assigned to duty in the Shenandoah Valley. Our gallant Captain still bears upon his face the mark of his meeting, in 1861, with Lieut., now Col., Kerchival West, who is also to serve in the valley, with Sheridan's Army. Another meeting between these two men would be one of the strange coincidences of the war, as they were at one time, if not indeed at present, interested in the same beautiful woman." (*Rises.*)

I will ask you to read the last few lines, yourself. (*X.-ing, hands* KER *the slip.*)

KER. (*Reading.*) "The scandal connected with the lovely wife of a Northern officer, at the opening of the war, was overshadowed, of course, by the attack on Fort Sumpter; but many Charlestonians will remember it. The lady in defense of whose good name Capt. Thornton fought the duel"—He defending her good name!— "is the wife of General Haverill, who will be Col. West's immediate commander." (*He pauses a moment, then hands back the slip.*) General! I struck Mr. Thornton after a personal quarrel.

HAV. And the cause of the blow? There is much more in this than I have ever known of. I need hardly say that I do not accept the statement of this scandalous paragraph as correct. I will ask you to tell me the whole story, frankly, as man to man.

KER. (*After a moment's thought.*) I will tell you—all—frankly, General.

[*Enter* SERGEANT BARKET, L. 3 E.]

BARKET. Colonel Wist? Adjutant Rollins wishes me to report—a prisoner—just captured.

HAVERILL. We will meet again later, to-night, when the camp is at rest. We are both soldiers, and have duties before us, at once. For the present, Colonel, be on the alert; we must watch the enemy. (*He moves up C.* BARKET *salutes.* HAVERILL *stops and looks at envelope in his hands, reading*) "Private and confidential." [*Exit,* L. 3 E.

KERCHIVAL. Sergeant Barket! Lieutenant Bedloe has crossed the enemy's lines, at Buckton's Ford, with a party of men. I wish you to ride to the ford yourself, and remain there, with your horse in readiness and fresh. As soon as any survivor of the party returns, ride back with the first news at full speed.

BARKET. Yes, sir. (*Starting.*)

KERCHIVAL. You say a prisoner has been captured? Is it a spy?

BARKET. Worse—a petticoat.

KER. (*Crossing* R.) A female prisoner! (*Dropping into seat,* R. C.)

BARKET. I towld the byes your honor wouldn't thank us fer the catchin' of her. The worst of it is she's a lady; and what's worse still, it's a purty one.

KER. Tell Major Wilson, for me, to let her take the oath, and everything else she wants. The Government of the United States will send her an apology and a new bonnet.

BARKET. The young lady is to take the oath, is it? She says she'll see us damned first.

KER. A lady, Barket?

BARKET. Well! she didn't use thim exact words. That's the way I understand her emphasis. Ivery time she looks at me, I feel like getting under a boom-proof. She was dashing through the woods on a gray horse, sur; and we had the divil's own chase. But we came up wid her, at last, down by the bend in Oak Run. Just at that moment we saw the figure of a Confederate officer, disapparing among the trays on the ither side.

KER. A—h!

BARKET. Two of us rayturned wid the girl; and the rist wint after the officer. Nothing has been heard of thim yet.

KER. Have you found any dispatches on the prisoner?

BARKET. Well!—yer honor, I'u a bachelor, meself; and I'm not familiar with the jayography of the sex. We byes are in mortal terror for fear somebody might order us to go on an exploring expedition.

KER. Tell them to send the prisoner here, Barket, and hurry to Buckton's Ford yourself, at once.

BARKET. As fast as me horse can carry me, sir, and it's a good one. [*Exit,* L. 3 E.

KER. I'd rather deal with half the Confederate army than with one woman, but I must question her. They captured her down by the Bend in Oak Run. (*Taking out map; looks at it.*) I see. She had just met, or was about to meet, a Confederate officer at that point. It is evident that she was either taking him a dispatch or was there to receive one. Oak Run. (CORPORAL DUNN *and two soldiers enter*, L. 3 E., *with* GERT. *as a prisoner. They stop*, C. KER. *sits, facing* R. *and studying map.* GERT. *glances at him and marches down* L. *with head erect; stops, with her back to him, down* L.)

CORP. DUNN. The prisoner, Colonel West!

KERCHIVAL. Ah! Very well, Corporal; you can go. (*Rising; he motions the guard to retire.* CORP. DUNN *gives the necessary orders and exit with guard,* L. 3 E.) Be seated, madame. GERT. *draws up, folding her arms and planting her foot, spitefully.* KER. *shrugs his shoulder. Aside.*) I wish they'd capture a tigress for me, or some other female animal that I know how to manage better than I do with a woman. (*Aloud.*) I am very sorry, madam; but, of course, my duty as a military officer is paramount to all other considerations. You have been captured within the lines of this army, and under circumstances which lead me to think that you have important despatches upon your person. I trust that you will give me whatever you have, at once. I shall be exceedingly sorry if you compel me to adopt the extreme—and the very disagreeable course—for both of us—of having you—I—I hesitate even to use the word, madame—but military law is absolute—having you——

GERT. Searched! If you dare, Colonel West! (*Turning to him suddenly and drawing up to her full height.*)

KER. Gertrude Ellingham! (*Springs across to her, with his arms extended.*) My dear Gertrude!

GERT. (*Turning her back upon him.*) Not "dear Gertrude" to you, sir!

KER. Not?—Oh! I forgot.

GERT. (*Coldly.*) I am your prisoner.

KER. Yes. (*Drawing up firmly, with a change of manner.*) We will return to the painful realities of war. I am very sorry that you have placed yourself in a position like this, and, believe me, Gertrude—(*With growing tenderness.*)—I am still more sorry to be in such a position myself. (*Resting one hand on her arm, and his other arm about her waist.*)

GERT. (*After looking down at his hands.*) You don't like the position? (*He starts back, drawing up with dignity.*) Is that the paramount duty of a military officer?

KER. You will please hand me whatever despatches or other papers may be in your possession.

GERT. (*Looking away.*) You will *force* me, I suppose. I am a woman; you have the power. Order in the guard! A Corporal and two men—you'd better make it a dozen—I am dangerous! Call the whole regiment to arms! Beat the long roll! I won't give up, if all the armies of the United States surround me.

[*Enter* GEN. BUCKTHORN, L. 3. E.]

KER. General Buckthorn! (*Saluting and* X.*-ing* R.)

BUCK. Col. West!

GERT. (*Aside.*) Jenny's father! (*Buckthorn glances at* GERT., *who still stands looking away,* L. *He moves down to* KERCHIVAL.)

BUCK. (*Apart, gruffly.*) I was passing with my staff, and I was informed that you had captured a woman bearing despatches to the enemy. Is this the one?

KER. Yes, General.

BUCK. Ah! (*Turning, looks at her.*)

GER. I wonder if he will recognize me. He hasn't seen me since I was a little girl. (*Turns toward him.*)

BUCK. (*Turning to* KER.; *punches him in the ribs.*) Fine young woman!—(*Turns and bows to her very gallantly, removing his hat. She bows deeply in return.*) A—h—e—m! (*Suddenly pulling himself up to a stern, military air; then gruffly to* KER., *extending his hand.*) Let me see the despatches.

KER. She declines positively to give them up.

BUCK. Oh! Does she? (*Walks up* C., *thoughtfully; turns.*) My dear young lady! I trust you will give us no further trouble. Kindly let us have those despatches.

GERT. (*Looking away* L.) I have no despatches, and I would not give them to you if I had.

BUCK. What! You defy my authority? Col. West, I command you! Search the prisoner! (GERTRUDE *turns suddenly towards* KER., *facing him defiantly. He looks across at her aghast. A moment's pause.*)

KER. General Buckthorn—I decline to obey that order.

BUCK. You—you decline to obey my order! (*Moves down to him fiercely.*)

KER. (*Apart.*) General! It is the woman I love.

BUCK. (*Apart.*) Is it? Damn you, sir! I wouldn't have an officer in my army corps who *would* obey me, under such circumstances. I'll have to look for those dispatches myself.

KER. (*Facing him, angrily.*) If you dare, General Buckthorn!

BUCK. (*Apart.*) Blast your eyes! I'd kick you out of the army if you'd *let* me search her; but it's my military duty to swear at you. (*To* GERTRUDE.) Col. West has sacrificed his life to protect you.

GERT. His life!

BUCK. I shall have him shot for insubordination to his commander, immediately. (*Gives* KER. a *huge wink, and turns up* R. C.)

GERT. Oh, sir! General! I have told you the truth. I have no despatches. Believe me, sir, I haven't so much as a piece of paper about me, except——

BUCK. Except? (*Turning sharply.*)

GERT. Only a letter. Here it is. (*Taking letter from the bosom of her dress.*) Upon my soul, it is all I have. Truly, it is.

BUCK. (*Taking letter.*) Col. West, you're reprieved. (*Winks at* KER., *who turns away, laughing.* BUCK *reads letter.*) "Washington"—Ho!—ho! From within our own lines!—"Colonel Kerchival West"——

KER. Eh?

GERT. Please, General!—Don't read it aloud.

BUCK. Very well! I won't.

KER. (*Aside.*) I wonder what it has to do with me.

BUCK. (*Reading. Aside.*) "If Kerchival West had heard you say, as I did—m—m——that you loved him with your whole heart—" (*He glances up at* GERTRUDE, *who drops her head, coyly.*) This is a very important military document. (*Turns to last page.*) "Signed, Constance Haverill." (*Turns to front page.*) "My dear Gertrude!" Is this Miss Gertrude Ellingham?

GERT. Yes, General.

BUCK. I sent my daughter Jenny to your house, with an escort, this morning.

GERT. She is here.

BUCK. (*Tapping her under the chin.*) You're an arrant little Rebel, my dear; but I like you immensely. (*Draws up suddenly, with an Ahem! Turns to* KERCHIVAL.) Colonel West, I leave this dangerous young woman in your charge. (KER. *approaches.*) If she disobeys you in any way, or attempts to escape—read that letter! (*Giving him the letter.*)

GERT. Oh! General!

BUCK. But not till then. (*X.-ing* R.)

KER. (*Tenderly, taking her hand.*) My—prisoner!

GERT. (*Aside.*) I could scratch my own eyes out—or his, either—rather than have him read that letter.

[*Enter* CORPORAL DUNN, L. U. E., *with Guard of four soldiers and* CAPT. EDWARD THORNTON *as a prisoner.*]

KER. Edward Thornton!

GERT. They have taken him, also! He has the despatch!

DUNN. The Confederate Officer, Colonel, who was pursued by our troops at Oak Run, after they captured the young lady.

BUCK. The little witch has been communicating with the enemy!

KER. (*To* GERT.) You will give me your parole of honor until we next meet?

GERT. Yes. (*Aside.*) That letter! I *am* his prisoner. (*She walks up the steps.* KER. *X.'s* R. GERT. *looks back at* THORNTON. *Exit* L.)

KER. (*X.'s* R. *to* BUCK.) We shall probably find the despatches we have been looking for now, General.

BUCK. Prisoner! You will hand us what papers you may have.

THORN. I will hand you nothing.

BUCK. Colonel! (KER. *motions to* THORN., *who looks at him sullenly. Bus. and moves down* L. C.)

KER. Corporal Dunn!—search the prisoner. (DUNN *steps to* THORNTON, *taking him by the shoulder and turning him rather roughly.* THORNTON'S *back to the audience.* DUNN *throws open his coat, takes paper from his breast, hands it to* KER., *who gives it to* BUCKTHORN.) Proceed with the search. (DUNN *continues the search.* BUCK. *drops upon seat,* R. C., *lights a match, looks at the paper.*)

BUCK. (*Reading.*) "General Rosser will rejoin General Early with all the cavalry in his command, at——" This is important. (*Continues to read with matches. The* CORPORAL *hands a packet to* KER. *He removes the covering.*)

KER. (*Starting.*) A portrait of Mrs. Haverill! (*He touches* COR. DUNN, *on the shoulder quickly and motions him to retire.* DUNN *falls back to the guard.* KER. *speaks apart to* THORNTON, *who has turned front.*) How did this portrait come into your possession?

THORN. That is my affair, not yours!

BUCK. Anything else, Colonel?

KER. (*Placing the miniature in his pocket.*) Nothing!

THORN. (*Apart, over* KERCHIVAL'S *shoulder.*) A time will come, perhaps, when I can avenge the insult of this search, and also this scar. (*Pointing to a scar on his face.*) Your aim was better than mine in Charleston, but we shall meet again; give me back that picture.

KER. Corporal! Take your prisoner!

THORN. Ah! (*Viciously springing at* KERCHIVAL; CORPORAL DUNN *springs forward, seizes* THORNTON *and throws him back to the Guard.* KERCHIVAL *walks* R., DUNN *stands with his carbine levelled at* THORNTON, *looks at* KERCHIVAL, *who quietly motions him out.* CORPORAL DUNN *gives the orders to the men and marches out,* L. 3 E., *with* THORNTON.)

BUCK. Ah! (*Still reading with matches.*) Colonel! (*Rising.*) The enemy has a new movement on foot, and General Sheridan has left the army! Listen! (*Reads from despatches with matches.*) " Watch for a signal from Three Top Mountain to-night."

KER. We hope to be able to read that signal ourselves.

BUCK. Yes, I know. Be on your guard. I will speak with Gen. Haverill, and then ride over to General Wright's headquarters. Keep us informed.

KER. I will, General. (*Saluting.* BUCKTHORN *salutes and exit,* L. 3. E.)

KER. " Watch for a signal from Three Top Mountain to-night." (*Looking up at Mountain.*) We shall be helpless to read it unless Lieut. Bedloe is successful. I only hope the poor boy is not lying dead, already, in those dark woods beyond the ford. (*Looking off* L. *from up* C.; *turns down, taking the miniature from his pocket.*) How came Edward Thornton to have this portrait of Mrs. Haverill in his possession? (GERTRUDE *runs in* L. 2 E., *on veranda.*)

GERT. Oh, Colonel West! He's here! (*Looks back.*) They are coming this way with him.

KER. Him! Who?

GERT. Jack.

KER. Jack!

GERT. My own horse!

KER. Ah, I remember! He and I were acquainted in Charleston.

GERT. Two troopers are passing through the camp with him.

KER. He is not in your possession?

GERT. He was captured at the battle of Fair Oaks, but I recognized him the moment I saw him; and I am sure he knew me, too, when I went up to him. He whinnied and looked so happy. You are in command here—(*Running down.*)—you will compel them to give him up to me?

KER. If he is in my command, your pet shall be returned to you. I'll give one of my own horses to the Government as a substitute, if necessary.

GERT. Oh, thank you, my dear Kerchival! (*Going to him; he takes her hand, looking into her eyes.*) I—I could almost——

KER. Can you almost confess, at last, Gertrude, that you—love me? (*Tenderly; she draws back, hanging her head, but leaving her hand in his.*) Have I been wrong? I felt that that confession was hovering on your tongue when we were separated in Charleston. Have I seen that confession in your eyes since we met again to-day—even among the angry flashes which they have shot out at me? During all this terrible war—in the camp and the trench—in the battle—I have dreamed of a meeting like this. You are still silent? (*Her hand is still in his. She is looking down. A smile steals over her face, and she raises her eyes to his, taking his hand in both her own.*)

GERT. Kerchival! (*Enter BENSON, L. 3 E. She looks around over her shoulder. KER. looks up L. A trooper leading the large black horse of Act 1st, now caparisoned in military saddle, bridle, etc., follows BENSON across; another trooper follows.*) Jack! (*She runs up stage, meeting horse, C. KER. turns R.*)

KER. Confound Jack! That infernal horse was always in my way!

GERT. (*With her arm about her horse's neck.*) My darling old fellow! Is he not beautiful, Kerchival? They have taken good care of him. How soft his coat is!

KER. Benson, explain this!

BENSON. I was instructed to show him through the lines, sir.

KER. What are your orders, my man? (*Moving up, the trooper hands him a paper. He moves a few steps down R. C., reading it.*)

GERT. You are to be mine again, Jack, mine! (*Resting her cheek against the horse's head and patting it.*) The Colonel has promised it to me.

KER. Ah! (*With a start, as he reads the paper. GERTRUDE raises her head and looks at him.*) This is General Sheridan's horse, on his way to Winchester, for the use of the General when he returns from Washington.

GERT. General Sheridan's horse? He is mine!

KER. I have no authority to detain him. He must go on.

GERT. I have hold of Jack's bridle, and you may order your men to take out their sabres and cut my hand off.

KER. (*He approaches her and gently takes her hand as it holds the bridle.*) I would rather have my own hand cut off, Gertrude, than bring tears to your eyes, but there is no alternative! (*GERT. releases the bridle and turns front, brushing her eyes, her hand still held in his, his back to the audience. He returns order and motions troopers out; they move out L., with horse. KER. turns to move R. GERT. starts after the horse; he turns quickly to check her.*) You forget—that—you are my prisoner!

GERT. I will go!

KER. General Buckthorn left me special instructions—(*taking out wallet and letter*)—in case you declined to obey my orders——

GERT. Oh, Colonel! Please don't read that letter. (*She stands near him, dropping her head. He glances up at her from the letter. She glances up at him and drops her eyes again.*) I will obey you. (*Walks to* L. C.)

KER. (*Aside.*) What the deuce can there be in that letter?

GERT. Colonel West! Your men made me a prisoner this afternoon; to-night you have robbed me, by your own order, of— of—Jack is only a pet, but I love him; and my brother is also a captive in your hands. When we separated in Charleston you said that we were enemies. What is there lacking to make those words true to-day? You *are* my enemy! A few moments ago you asked me to make a confession to you. You can judge for yourself whether it is likely to be a confession of—love—or of hatred!

KER. Hatred! (*X.-ing to her.*)

GERT. (*Facing him.*) Listen to my confession, sir! From the bottom of my heart——

.KER. Stop!

GERT. I will not stop!

KER. I command you.

GERT. Indeed! (*He throws open the wallet in his hand and raises the letter.*) Ah! (*She turns away; turns again, as if to speak. He half opens the letter. She stamps her foot and walks up steps of the veranda. Here she turns again.*) I tell you, I——(*He opens the letter. She turns, and exit with spiteful step,* L. 2 E.)

KER. I wonder if that document orders me to cut her head off! (*Returning it to wallet and pocket.*) Was ever lover in such a position? I am obliged to cross the woman I love at every step.

[*Enter* CORPORAL DUNN, L. 3 E., *very hurriedly.*]

DUNN. A message from Adjutant Rollins, sir! The prisoner, Capt. Thornton, dashed away from the special guard which was placed over him, and he has escaped. He had a knife concealed, and two of the Guard are badly wounded. Adjutant Rollins thinks the prisoner is still within the lines of the camp—in one of the houses or the stables.

KER. Tell Major Wilson to place the remainder of the Guard under arrest, and to take every possible means to recapture the prisoner. (*CORP.* DUNN *salutes, and exit* L. 3 E.) So! Thornton has jumped his guard, and he is armed. I wonder if he is trying to get away, or to find me. From what I know of the man, he doesn't much care which he succeeds in doing. That scar which I gave him in Charleston is deeper in his heart than it is in his face. (*A signal light suddenly appears on Three Top Mountain. The "Call."*) Ah!—the enemy's signal! (*Enter* CAPT. LOCK-WOOD, L. 3 E., *followed by* LIEUT. OF SIGNAL CORPS.) Capt. Lock-wood! You are here! Are your Signalmen with you?

LOCK. Yes, Colonel; and one of my Lieutenants. (*The* LIEUT. *is looking up at signal with glass.* CAPT. LOCKWOOD *does the same.* HAVERILL *enters* L. 3 E., *followed by two Staff Officers.*)

HAVER. (*As he enters up* L. C.) Can you make anything of it, Captain?

LOCKWOOD. Nothing, General! Our services are quite useless unless Lieut. Bedloe returns with the key to their signals.

HAVER. A—h! (*Coming down* L. C.) We shall fail. It is time he had returned, if successful.

SENTINEL. (*Without,* L.) Halt! Who goes there? (KER. *runs up stage* C., *and half way up incline,* R. C., *looking off* L.) Halt! (*A shot without,* L.)

BARKET. (*Without.*) Och!—Ye murthern spalpeen!

KER. (*Up* L. C.) Sentinel! Let him pass; it is Sergeant Barket.

SENTINEL. (*Without.*) Pass on.

KER. He didn't give the countersign. News from Lieutenant Bedloe, General!

BARKET. (*Hurrying in, up slope,* L.) Col. Wist, our brave byes wiped out the enemy, and here's the papers.

KER. Ah! (*Taking papers. Then to* LOCKWOOD.) Is that the key?

LOCK. Yes, Lieutenant! (LIEUT. *hurries up to elevation, looking through his glass.* LOCKWOOD *opens book.*)

HAVER. What of Lieut. Bedloe, Sergeant?

BARKET. Sayreously wounded, and in the hands of the inimy!

HAVER. (*Sighing.*) A—h!

BARKET. (*Coming down stone steps*) It is repoted that Capt. Heartsaze was shot dead at his side.

KER. Heartsease dead! (*Moves down* R. C.)

LIEUT. OF SIGNAL CORPS. (*Reading Signals.*) Twelve—Twenty-two—Eleven (12, 2211, 3.)

BARKET. Begorra! I forgot the Sintinil entirely, but he didn't forget me. (*Holding his left arm.*)

HAVER. Colonel West! We must make every possible sacrifice for the immediate exchange of Lieut. Bedloe, if he is still living. It is due to him. Col. Robert Ellingham is a prisoner in this camp; offer him his own exchange for young Bedloe.

KER. He will accept, of course. I will ride to the front with him myself, General, and show him through the lines.

HAVER. At once! (KER. *crosses front and exit on veranda,* L. 2 E. HAVERILL *crosses* R.) Can you follow the despatch, Captain?

LOCK. Perfectly; everything is here.

HAVER. Well!

LIEUT. OF SIGNAL CORPS. Eleven—Twenty-two—One—Twelve. (11, 22, 112, 3.)

LOCK. (*From book.*) "General Longstreet is coming with——"

HAVER. Longstreet!

LIEUT. OF SIGNAL CORPS. One—Twenty-one. (1, 21, 33.)

LOCK. "With eighteen thousand men."

HAVER. Longstreet and his corps!

LIEUT. OF SIGNAL CORPS. Two—Eleven—Twenty-two. (211, 22, 33.)

LOCK. "Sheridan is away!"

HAVER. They have discovered his absence!

LIEUT. OF SIGNAL CORPS. Two—Twenty-two—Eleven—One—Twelve—One. (222, 11, 3, 112, 1, 333.)

LOCK. "We will crush the Union Army before he can return."

HAVER. Signal that despatch from here to our Station at Front Royal. (*Pointing* R.) Tell them to send it after General Sheridan—and ride for their lives. (LOCKWOOD *hurries out* L. 3 E.) Major Burton! We will ride to General Wright's headquarters at once—our horses! (*Moving up* C. *Noise of a struggle without*, L.)

BARKET. (*Looking* L.) What the devil is the row out there? (*Exit*, L. 3. E. *Also one of the Staff Officers.*)

HAVER. (C., *Looking off* L.) What is this! Colonel West wounded!

[*Enter* KERCHIVAL WEST, L. 3 E., *his coat thrown open, with* ELLINGHAM, BARKET *assisting.*]

ELLING. Steady, Kerchival, old boy! You should have let us carryyou.

KER. Nonsense, old fellow! It's a mere touch with the point of the knife. I—I'm faint—with the loss of a little blood—that's all. Bob!—I——(*Reels suddenly and is caught by* ELLINGHAM *as he sinks to the ground, insensible.*)

ELLING. Kerchival! (*Kneeling at his side.*)

HAVER. (*Moving* L.) Go for the Surgeon! (*To Staff Officer, who goes out quickly on veranda*, L. 2. E.) How did this happen? (*Enter* CORPORAL DUNN *and Guard*, L. 2 E., *with* THORNTON. *He is in his shirt sleeves and disheveled, his arms folded. They march down* R.) Captain Thornton!

ELLING. We were leaving the house together; a hunted animal sprang suddenly across our path, like a panther. (*Looking over his shoulder.*) There it stands. Kerchival!—my brother!

CORP. DUNN. We had just brought this prisoner to bay, but I'm afraid we were too late.

HAVER. This is assassination, sir, not war. If you have killed him——

THORN. Do what you like with me; we need waste no words. I had an old account to settle, and I have paid my debt.

ELLING. General Haverill! I took these from his breast when he first fell. (*Handing up wallet and miniature to* HAVERILL. HAVERILL *starts as he looks at the miniature.* THORNTON watches him.)

HAVER. (*Aside.*) My wife's portrait!

THORN. If I have killed him—your honor will be buried in the same grave.

HAVER. Her picture on his breast! She gave it to him—not to my son! (*Dropping into seat*, R. C. CAPT. LOCKWOOD *enters with a Signalman, who has a burning torch on a long pole; he hurries up the elevation.* CAPT. LOCKWOOD *stands below*, R. C., *facing him. Almost simultaneously with the entrance of the Signalman,* GERTRUDE *runs in on veranda*, L. 2 E.)

GERT. They are calling for a surgeon! Who is it? Brother!—you are safe, Ah! (*Uttering a scream, as she sees* KERCHIVAL, *and falling on her knees at his side.*) Kerchival! Forget those last bitter words I said to you. Can't you hear my confession? I do love you. Can't you hear me? I love you! (*The Signalman is swinging the torch as the curtain descends*, LOCKWOOD *looking* R.)

CURTAIN.

ACT III.

SCENE.—*Same. It is now bright daylight, with sunshine flecking the foreground and bathing the distant valley and mountains.*

DISCOVERED.—JENNY, *on low stone post, c., looking* L. *As the curtain rises, she imitates Trumpet Signal No. 19 on her closed fists.*

JENNY. What a magnificent line! (*Looking* L.) Guides-posts! Every man and every horse is eager for the next command. There comes the flag! (*Trumpet Signal without, No. 30.*) To the standard! (*As the signal begins.*) The regiment is going to the front. Oh! I do wish I could go with it. I always do, the moment I hear the trumpets. Boots and saddles! (*Imitates No. 16.*) Mount! (*Imitates No. 37.*) I wish I was in command of the regiment. It was born in me. (*Trumpet Signal No. 48, without.*) Fours right! There they go! Look at those horses' ears! (*Trumpet Signal No. 39, without.*) Forward. (*Military band heard without—"The Battle Cry of Freedom."* (JENNY *takes attitude of holding bridle and trotting.*) Rappity—plap—plap—plap, etc. (*She imitates the motions of a soldier on horse-back, stepping down to rock at side of post; thence to ground and about stage, with the various curvettings of a spirited horse. Chorus of soldiers without, R., with the band. The music becomes more and more distant.* JENNY *gradually stops as the music is dying away, and stands, listening. As it dies entirely away, she suddenly starts to an enthusiastic attitude.*) Ah! If I were only a man! The enemy! On Third Battalion, left, front, into line, march! Draw sabres! Charge! (*Imitates Trumpet Signal No. 44. As she finishes, she rises to her full height, with both arms raised, and trembling with enthusiasm.*) Ah! (*She suddenly drops her arms and changes to an attitude and expression of disappointment—pouting.*) And the first time Old Margery took me to papa, in her arms, she had to tell him I was a girl. Papa was as much disgusted as I was. But he'd never admit it; he says I'm as good a soldier as any of 'em—just as I am.

[*Enter* BARKET, L. 2 E., *on veranda, his arm in a sling.*]

BARKET. (*On veranda.*) Miss Jenny!

JENNY. Barket! The regiment has marched away to the front, and we girls are left here, with just you and a corporal's guard to look after us.

BARKET. I've been watching the byes mesilf. (*Coming down.*) If a little milithary sugar-plum like you, Miss Jenny, objects to not goin' wid' em, what do you think of an ould piece of hard tack like me? I can't join the regiment till I've taken you and Miss Madeline back to Winchester, by your father's orders. But it isn't the first time I've escorted you, Miss Jenny. Many a time, when you was a baby, on the Plains, I commanded a special guard to accompany ye's from one fort to anither, and we gave the command in a whisper, so as not to wake ye's up.

JENNY. I told you to tell papa that I'd let him know when Madeline and I were ready to go.

BARKET. I tould him that I'd as soon move a train of army mules.

JENNY. I suppose we must start for home again to-day?

BARKET. Yes, Miss Jenny, in charge of an ould Sargeant wid his arm in a sling and a couple of convalescent throopers. This department of the United States Army will move to the rear in half an hour.

JENNY. Madeline and I only came yesterday morning.

BARKET. Whin your father got ye's a pass to the front, we all thought the fightin' in the Shenandoey Valley was over. It looks now as if it was just beginning. This is no place for women, now. Miss Gertrude Ellingham ought to go wid us, but she won't.

JENNY. Barket! Captain Heartsease left the regiment yesterday, and he hasn't rejoined it; he isn't with them, now, at the head of his company. Where is he?

BARKET. I can't say where he is, Miss Jenny. (*Aside.*) Lyin' unburied in the woods, where he was shot, I'm afraid.

JENNY. When Captain Heartsease does rejoin the regiment, Barket (*X.-ing L.*), please say to him for me, that,—that I—I may have some orders for him, when we next meet.

[*Exit, L. 2 E., on veranda.*

BARKET. Whin they nixt mate. They tell us there is no such thing as marriage in Hiven. If Miss Jenny and Capt. Heartsease mate there, they'll invint somethin' that's mighty like it. While I was lyin' wounded in General Buckthorn's house at Washington, last summer, and ould Margery was taking care of me, Margery tould me, confidentially, that they was in love wid aitch ither; and I think she was about right. I've often seen Captain Heartsease take a sly look at a little lace handkerchief, just before we wint into battle. (*Looks off L.*) Here's General Buckthorn himself. He and I must make it as aisy as we can for Miss Jenny's poor heart.

[*Enter GENERAL BUCKTHORN, L. 3 E.*]

BUCK. Sergeant Barket! You haven't started with those girls yet?

BARKET. They're to go in half an hour, sir.

BUCK. Be sure they do go. Is General Haverill here?

BARKET. Yes, sir; in the house with some of his staff, and the Surgeon.

BUCK. Ah! The Surgeon. How is Colonel West, this morning, after the wound he received last night?

BARKET. He says, himself, that he's as well as iver he was; but the Colonel and Surgeon don't agray on that subject. The dochter says he musn't lave his room for a month. The knife wint dape; and there's somethin' wrong inside of him. But the Colonel, bein' on the outside himsilf, can't see it. He's as cross as a bear, baycause they wouldn't let him go to the front this morning, at the head of his regiment. I happened to raymark that the Chaplain was prayin' for his raycovery. The Colonel said he'd court-martial him if he didn't stop that—quick; there's more important things for the Chaplain to pray for in his official capacity. Just at that moment the trumpets sounded, " Boots and Saddles." I had to dodge one of his boots, and the Surgeon had a narrow escape from the ither one. It was lucky for us both his saddle wasn't in the room.

BUCK. That looks encouraging. I think Kerchival will get on. (*X.-ing* L.)

BARKET. Might I say a word to you, sur, about Miss Jenny?

BUCK. Certainly, Barket. You and old Margery and myself have been a sort of triangular mother, so to speak, to the little girl—(*X.-ing to him.*)—since her own poor mother left her to our care, when she was only a baby, in the old fort on the Plains. (*At his side and unconsciously resting his arm over* BARKET'S *shoulder, familiarly. Suddenly draws up.*) Ahem! (*Then gruffly.*) What is it? Proceed.

BARKET. Her mother's bosom would have been the softest place for her poor little head to rest upon, now, sur.

BUCK. (*Touching his eyes.*) Well!

BARKET. Ould Margery tould me in Washington that Miss Jenny and Captain Heartsease were in love wid aitch ither.

BUCK. (*Starting.*) In love!

BARKET. I approved of the match.

BUCK. What the devil! (BARKET *salutes quickly and starts up stage and out* L. BUCK. *moves up after him; stops at post,* R. C. BARKET *stops in road,* L. C.)

BARKET. So did ould Margery.

BUCK. March! (*Angrily.* BARKET *salutes suddenly, and exit* L. 3 E.) Heartsease! That young jackanapes! A mere fop; he'll never make a soldier. My girl in love with—bah! I don't believe it; she's too good a soldier, herself.

[*Enter* HAVERILL, L. 2 E., *on veranda.*]

Ah, Haverill!

HAVER. Gen. Buckthorn! Have you heard anything of Gen. Sheridan since I sent that despatch to him last evening?

BUCK. He received it at midnight and sent back word that he considers it a ruse of the enemy. General Wright agrees with him. The reconnoissance yesterday showed no hostile force on our right, and Crook reports that Early is retreating up the valley. But Gen. Sheridan may, perhaps, give up his journey to Washington, and he has ordered some changes in our line, to be executed this afternoon at four o'clock. I rode over to give you your instructions in person. You may order Gen. MaCuen to go into camp on the right of Meadow Brook, with the second division. (*Haverill is writing in his note-book.*)

[*Enter* JENNY, L. 2 E., *on veranda.*]

JENNY. Oh, papa! I'm so glad you've come. I've got something to say to you. (*Running down and jumping into his arms, kissing him. He turns with her, and sets her down,* R. C., *squarely on her feet and straight before him.*)

BUCK. And I've got something to say to you—about Captain Heartsease.

JENNY. Oh! That's just what I wanted to talk about.

BUCK. Fall in! Front face! (*She jumps into military position, turning towards him.*) What's this I hear from Sergeant Barket? He says you've been falling in love.

JENNY. I have. (*Saluting.*)

BUCK. Young woman! Listen to my orders. Fall out! (*Turns sharply and marches to* HAVERILL.) Order the Third Brigade of Cavalry, under Col. Lowell, to occupy the left of the pike.

JENNY. Papa! (*Running to him and seizing the tail of his coat.*) Papa, dear!

BUCK. Close in Col. Powell on the extreme left—(*slapping his coat-tails out of* JENNY's *hands, without looking around*)—and hold Custer on the second line, at Old Forge Road. That is all at present. (*Turns to* JENNY.) Good bye, my darling! (*Kisses her.*) Remember your orders! You little pet! (*Chuckling, as he taps her chin; draws up suddenly; turns to* HAVERILL.) General! I bid you good-day.

HAVER. Good-day, Gen. Buckthorn. (*They salute with great dignity.* BUCK. *starts up stage;* JENNY *springs after him, seizing his coat-tails.*)

JENNY. But I want to talk with you, papa; I can't fall out. I—I—haven't finished yet. (*Etc., clinging to his coat, as* BUCK *marches out rapidly.* L. 3 E., *in road, holding back with all her might.*)

HAVER. It may have been a ruse of the enemy, but I hope that Gen. Sheridan has turned back from Washington. (*Moving L., looking at his note-book.*) We are to make changes in our line at four o'clock this afternoon. (*Returns book to pocket and stands in thought.*) The Surgeon tells me that Kerchival West will get on well enough if he remains quiet; otherwise not. He shall not die by the hand of a common assassin; he has no right to die like that. My wife gave my own picture of herself to him—not to my son—and she looked so like an angel when she took it from my hand! They were both false to me, and they have been true to each other. I will save his life for myself.

[*Enter* GERTRUDE, L. 2 E., *on veranda.*]

GERT. Gen. Haverill! (*Anxiously, coming down.*) Col. West persists in disobeying the injunctions of the Surgeon. He is preparing to join his regiment at the front. Give him your orders to remain here. Compel him to be prudent!

HAVER. (*Quickly.*) The honor of death at the front is not in reserve for him.

GERT. Eh? What did you say, General?

HAVER. Gertrude! I wish to speak to you, as your father's old friend; and I was once your guardian. Your father was my senior officer in the Mexican War. Without his care I should have been left dead in a foreign land. He, himself, afterwards fell fighting for the old flag.

GERT. The old flag. (*Aside.*) My father died for it, and he— (*looking L.*)—is suffering for it—the old flag!

HAVER. I can now return the kindness your father did to me, by protecting his daughter from something that may be worse than death.

GERT. What do you mean?

HAVER. Last night I saw you kneeling at the side of Kerchival West; you spoke to him with all the tender passion of a Southern woman. You said you loved him. But you spoke into ears that could not hear you. Has he ever heard those words from your lips? Have you ever confessed your love to him before?

GERT. Never. Why do you ask?

HAVER. Do not repeat those words. Keep your heart to yourself, my girl.

GERT. General! Why do you say this to me? And at such a moment—when his life——

HAVER. His life! (*Turning sharply.*) It belongs to me!

GERT.—Oh!

KER. Sergeant! (*Without. He steps in, L. 3 E., in road, looking back.* GERTRUDE *X.-s up* L. C. HAVERILL *comes down* R.) See that my horse is ready at once. General! (*Saluting.*) Are there any orders for my regiment beyond those given to Major Wilson, in my absence, this morning? I am about to ride on after the troops and re-assume my command.

HAVER. (*Quietly.*) It is my wish, Colonel, that you remain here under the care of the Surgeon.

KER. My wound is a mere trifle. This may be a critical moment in the campaign, and I cannot rest here. I must be with my own men.

HAVER. (*Quietly.*) I beg to repeat the wish I have already expressed. (KERCHIVAL *walks to him, and speaks apart, almost under his breath, but very earnest in tone.*)

KER. I have had no opportunity, yet, to explain certain matters, as you requested me to do yesterday; but whatever there may be between us, you are now interfering with my duty and my privilege as a soldier; and it is my right to be at the head of my regiment.

HAVER. (*Quietly.*) It is my positive order that you do not re-assume your command.

KER. General Haverill, I protest against this——

HAVER. (*Quietly.*) You are under arrest, sir.

KER. Arrest!

GERT. Ah! (KER. *unclasps his belt and offers his sword to* HAVER.)

HAVER. (*Quietly.*) Keep your sword; I have no desire to humiliate you; but hold yourself subject to further orders from me. (KER. *moves* L. *and goes up veranda.*)

KER. (*X.-ing* L. *to veranda.*) My regiment at the front!—and I under arrest!   [*Exit* L. 3 E.

HAVER. Gertrude! If your heart refuses to be silent—if you feel that you must confess your love to that man—first tell him what I have said to you, and refer him to me for an explanation.
                    [*Exit up* C. *and out* L. 3 E., *in road.*

GERT. (*N.-ing* R. C.) What can he mean? He would save me from something worse than death, he said. "His life—It belongs to me!" What can he mean? Kerchival told me that he loved me—it seems many years since that morning in Charleston—and when we met again. yesterday, he said that he had never ceased to love me. I will not believe that he has told me a falsehood. I have given him my love, my whole soul and my faith. (*Drawing up to her full height.*) My perfect faith! (JENNY *runs in*, L. 3 E., *in road, and up the slope*, R. C. *She looks down the hill, up* L. JENNY *enters.*)

JENNY. A flag of truce, Gertrude. And a party of Confederate soldiers, with an escort, coming up the hill. They are carrying someone; he is wounded.

(*Enter*, L. 4 E., *up the slope, a Lieutenant of Infantry with an escort of Union Soldiers, their arms at right shoulder, and a party of Confederate Soldiers bearing a rustic stretcher.* LIEUTENANT FRANK BEDLOE *lies on the stretcher.* MAJOR HARDWICK, *a Confederate Surgeon, walks at his side.* MADELINE *appears at veranda, from* L. 2 E., *watching them.* JENNY *moves down* L. GERTRUDE *stands with her back to audience, down* R. *The Lieutenant gives orders in a low tone, and the front escort moves to* R., *in road. The Confederate bearers and the Surgeon pass through the gate*, C. *The rear escort moves to* L. C., *in road, under Lieutenant's orders. The bearers halt, front; on a sign from the Surgeon, leave the stretcher on the ground, stepping back*, R. & L.)

MAJ. HARD. Is General Haverill here?

GERT. Yes; what can we do, sir?

MAD. The General is just about mounting with his staff, to ride away. Shall I go for him, sir?

MAJ. Say to him, please, that Colonel Robert Ellingham, of the Tenth Virginia, sends his respects and sympathy. He instructed me to bring this young officer to this point. in exchange for himself, as agreed upon between them last evening.

[*Exit* MADELINE, L. 2. E.

JENNY. Is he unconscious or sleeping, sir?

MAJ. Hovering between life and death. I thought he would bear the removal better. He is waking. Here, my lad! (*Placing his canteen to the lips of* FRANK, *who moves, reviving.*) We have reached the end of our journey.

FRANK. My father!

MAJ. He is thinking of his home. (FRANK *rises on one arm, assisted by the Surgeon.*)

FRANK. I have obeyed Gen. Haverill's orders, and I have a report to make.

GERT. We have already sent for him. (*Stepping to him.*) He will be here in a moment.

FRANK. (*Looking into her face, brightly.*) Is not this—Miss—Gertrude Ellingham?

GERT. You know me? You have seen me before?

FRANK. Long ago! Long ago! You know the wife of General Haverill?

GERT. I have no dearer friend in the world.

FRANK. She will give a message for me to the dearest friend *I* have in the world. My little wife! I must not waste even the moment we are waiting. Doctor! My note-book! (*Trying to get it from his coat. The Surgeon takes it out. A torn and blood-stained lace handkerchief also falls out.* GERT. *kneels at his side.*) Ah! I—I—have a message from another—(*Holding up hand-kerchief.*)—from Capt. Heartsease. (JENNY *makes a quick start towards him.*) He lay at my side in the hospital, when they brought me away; he had only strength enough to put this in my hand, and he spoke a woman's name; but I—I—forgot what it is. The red spots upon it are the only message he sent. (GERT. *takes the handkerchief and looks back at* JENNY, *extending her hand.* JENNY *moves to her, takes the handkerchief and turns back,* L., *looking down on it. She drops her face into her hands and goes out sobbing,* L. 2 E., *on veranda.*)

[*Enter* MADELINE *on veranda,* L. 2 E.]

MAD. General Haverill is coming. I was just in time. He was already on his horse.

FRANK. Ah! He is coming. (*Then suddenly.*) Write! Write! (GERT. *writes in the note-book as he dictates.*) "To—my wife—Edith:—Tell our little son, when he is old enough to know—how his father died; not how he lived. And tell her who filled my own mother's place so lovingly—she is your mother, too —that my father's portrait of her, which she gave to me in Charleston, helped me to be a better man!" And—Oh! I must not forget this—"It was taken away from me while I was a prisoner in Richmond, and it is in the possession of Capt. Henry Thornton, of the Confederate Secret Service. But her face is still beside your own in my heart. My best—warmest, last—love —to you, darling." I will sign it. (GERT. *holds the book, and he signs it, then sinks back very quietly, supported by the Surgeon.* GERT. *rises and walks* R.)

MAD. Gen. Haverill is here. (*The Surgeon lays the fold of the blanket over* FRANK'S *face and rises.*)

GERT. Doctor!

MAJ. He is dead. (MADELINE, *on veranda, turns and looks* L. *The Lieutenant orders the guard,* "Present Arms." *Enter* HAVERILL, L. 2 E., *on veranda. He salutes the guard as he passes. The Lieutenant orders,* "Carry Arms." HAVERILL *comes down* L. C.)

HAVER. I am too late?

MAJ. I'm sorry, General. His one eager thought as we came was to reach here in time to see you. (HAVERILL *moves to the bier, looks down at it, then folds back the blanket from the face. He starts slightly as he first sees it.*)

HAVER. The brave boy! I hoped once to have a son like you. I shall be in your father's place, to-day, at your grave. (*He replaces the blanket and steps back,* L. C.) We will carry him to his comrades in the front. He shall have a soldier's burial, in sight of the mountain-top beneath which he sacrificed his young life; that shall be his monument.

MAJ. Pardon me. General. We Virginians are your enemies, but you cannot honor this young soldier more than we do. Will you allow my men the privilege of carrying him to his grave? (HAVERILL *inclines his head. The Surgeon motions to the Confederate Soldiers, who step to the bier and raise it gently.*)

HAVER. Lieutenant! (*The Lieutenant orders the guard, "Left Face." The Confederate bearers move through the gate, preceded by* LIEUTENANT HARDWICK. HAVERILL *draws his sword, reverses it, and moves up behind the bier with bowed head. The Lieutenant orders "Forward March," and the cortege disappears. While the girls are still watching it, the heavy sound of distant artillery is heard, with booming reverberations among the hills and in the valley.*)

MAD. What is that sound, Gertrude?

GERT. Listen! (*Another and more prolonged distant sound, with long reverberations.*)

MAD. Again! Gertrude! (GERT. *raises her hand to command silence; listens. Distant cannon again.*)

GERT. It is the opening of a battle.

MAD. Ah! (*Running down stage,* L. C. *The sounds again. Prolonged rumble.*)

GERT. How often have I heard that sound! (*Coming down* R.) This is war, Madeline! You are face to face with it now.

MAD. And Robert is there! He may be in the thickest of the danger—at this very moment.

GERT. Yes. Let our prayers go up for him; mine do, with all a sister's heart. (KER. *enters on veranda,* L. 2 E., *without coat or vest, his sash about his waist, looking back as he comes in.*) Kerchival!

KER. Go on! Go on! Keep the battle to yourselves. I'm out of it. (*The distant cannon and reverberations rising in volume. Prolonged and distant rumble.*)

MAD. (L. C.) I pray for Robert Ellingham—and for the *cause* in which he risks his life! (KER. *looks at her, suddenly; also* GERT.) Heaven forgive me if I am wrong, but I am praying for the enemies of my country. His people are my people, his enemies are my enemies. Heaven defend him and his, in this awful hour.

KER. Madeline! My sister!

MAD. Oh, Kerchival! (*Turning and dropping her face on his breast.*) I cannot help it—I cannot help it!

KER. My poor girl! Every woman's heart, the world over, belongs not to any country or any flag, but to her husband—and her lover. Pray for the man you love, sister—it would be treason not to. (*Passes her before him to* L. *Looks across to* GERT.) Am I right? (GERT. *drops her head.* MAD. *moves up veranda and out,* K. 2 E.) Is what I have just said to Madeline true?

GERT. Yes! (*Looks up.*) Kerchival!

KER. Gertrude! (*Hurries across to her, clasps her in his arms. He suddenly staggers and brings his hand to his breast.*)

GERT. Your wound! (*Supporting him as he reels and sinks into seat,* R. C.)

KER. Wound! I have no wound! You do love me! (*Seizing her hand.*)

GERT. Let me call the Surgeon, Kerchival.

KER. You can be of more service to me than he can. (*Detaining her. Very heavy sounds of the battle ; she starts, listening.*) Never mind that ! It's only a battle. You love me!

GERT. Be quiet, Kerchival, dear. I do love you. I told you so, when you lay bleeding here, last night. But you could not hear me. (*At his side, resting her arm about him, stroking his head.*) I said that same thing to—to—another, more than three years ago. It is in that letter that General Buckthorn gave you. (KER. *starts.*) No—no—you must be very quiet, or I will not say another word. If you obey me, I will repeat that part of the letter, every word; I know it by heart, for I read it a dozen times. The letter is from Mrs. Haverill.

KER. (*Quietly.*) Go on.

GERT. "I have kept your secret, my darling, but I was sorely tempted to betray the confidence you reposed in me at Charleston. If Kerchival West—(*she retires backward from him as she proceeds*)—had heard you say, as I did, when your face was hidden in my bosom, that night, that you loved him with your whole heart——"

KER. Ah ! (*Starting to his feet. He sinks back. She springs to support him.*)

GERT. I will go for help.

KER. Do not leave me at such a moment as this. You have brought me a new life. (*Bringing her to her knees before him and looking down at her.*) Heaven is just opening before me. (*His hands drop suddenly and his head falls back. Battle.*)

GERT. Ah ! Kerchival ! You are dying ! (*Musketry. A sudden sharp burst of musketry, mingled with the roar of artillery near by* R. KERCHIVAL *starts, seizing* GERTRUDE'S *arm and holding her away,* R., *still on her knees. He looks eagerly,* L.)

KER. The enemy is close upon us !

[BARKET *runs in, up the slope,* L. 4 E.]

BARKET. Colonel West ! The devils have sprung out of the ground. They're pouring over our lift plank like Noah's own flood. The Union Army has started back for Winchester, on its way to the North Pole ; our own rigiment, Colonel, is coming over the hill in full retrate.

KER. My own regiment! (*Starting up.*) Get my horse, Barket. (*Turns.*) Gertrude, my life! (*Embraces* GERTRUDE.)

BARKET. Your horse is it? I'm wid ye! There's a row at Finnegan's ball, and we're in it. (*Springs to road,* L. C., *and out,* L. 3 E.)

KER. (*Turns away. Stops.*) I am under arrest. (*Retreat. Fugitives begin to straggle across stage from* L. 3 E.)

GERT. You must not go, Kerchival; it will kill you.

KER. Arrest be damned! (*Starts up* C., *raises his arms above his head with clenched fist, rising to full height.*) Stand out of my way, you cowards! (*They cower away from him as he rushes out among them, L. 3. E. The stream of fugitives passing across stage swells in volume.* GERTRUDE *runs through them and up to the elevation, turning.*)

GERT. Men! Are you soldiers? Turn back! There is a leader for you! Turn back! Fight for your flag—and mine; the flag my father died for! Turn back! (*She looks out L. and turns front.*) He has been marked for death already, and I—I only can pray. (*Dropping to her knees.*)

(*The stream of fugitives continues, now over the elevation also. Rough and torn uniforms, bandaged arms and legs; some limping and supported by others, some dragging their muskets after them, others without muskets, others using them as crutches. Variety of uniforms, cavalry, infantry, etc.; flags draggled on the ground, the rattle of near musketry and roar of cannon continue; two or three wounded fugitives drop down beside the hedge.* BENSON *staggers in and drops upon rock or stumps near post,* C. *Artillerists, rough, torn and wounded, drag and force a field-piece across.* CORPORAL DUNN, *wounded, staggers to the top of elevation. There is a lull in the sounds of the battle. Distant cheers are heard without,* R.)

DUNN. Listen, fellows! Stop! Listen! Sheridan! General Sheridan is coming! (*Cheers from those on stage.* GERTRUDE *rises quickly. The wounded soldiers rise, looking over hedge. All on stage stop, looking* L., *eagerly. The cheers without come nearer, with shouts of "Sheridan! Sheridan!"*) The horse is down; he is worn out.

GERT. No! He is up again! He is on my Jack! Now, for your life, Jack, and for me! You've never failed me yet. (*The cheers without now swell to full volume and are taken up by those on the stage. The horse sweeps by with General Sheridan.*) Jack! Jack!! Jack!!! (*Waving her arms as he passes. She throws up her arms and falls backward, caught by* DUNN. *The stream of men is reversed and surges across stage to* L., *in road and on elevation, with shouts, throwing up hats, etc. The field-piece is forced up the slope with a few bold, rough movements; the artillerists are loading it, and the stream of returning fugitives are still surging by in the road as the curtain falls.*)

CURTAIN.

ACT IV.

SCENE.—*Residence of* GENERAL BUCKTHORN, *in Washington.
Interior. Fireplace slanting upward from* L. C. *to* C. *Small
alcove up* R. C. *Opening to hall up* L. C., *with staircase beyond,
and also entrance from out* L. *Door up* R. *A wide opening,
with portieres,* L. 2 E., *to apartment. Upright piano down* R.
Armchair and low stool before fireplace, C. *Small table up*
L. C., *for tea, etc. Ottoman,* R. C. *Other chairs, ottoms. &c.,
to taste.*

TIME.—*Afternoon.*

DISCOVERED.—MRS. HAVERILL, *in armchair, resting her face
upon her hand, and looking into the fire.* EDITH *is on a low
stool at her side, sewing a child's garment.*

EDITH.—It seems hardly possible that the war is over, and that
General Lee has really surrendered. (*Fife and drum, without.*)
There is music in the streets nearly all the time, now, and everybody looks so cheerful and bright. (*Distant fife and drums heard
playing "Johnnie Comes Marching Home."* EDITH *springs up and
runs up to window, looking out.*) More troops returning! The old,
tattered battle-flag is waving in the wind, and people are running
after them so merrily. (*Music stops.*) Every day, now, seems
like a holiday. (*Coming down.*) The war is over. All the
women ought to feel very happy, whose—whose husbands are—
coming back to them.
    MRS. H. Yes, Edith; those women whose—husbands are com-
ing back to them. (*Still looking into fire.*)
    EDITH. Oh! (*Dropping upon the stool, her head upon the arm
of the chair.*)
    MRS. H. (*Resting her arm over her.*) My poor, little darling!
Your husband will not come back.
    EDITH. Frank's last message has never reached me.
    MRS. H. No; but you have one sweet thought always with
you. Madeline West heard part of it, as Gertrude wrote it down.
His last thought was a loving one, of you.
    EDITH. Madeline says that he was thinking of you, too. He
knew that you were taking such loving care of his little one, and
of me. You have always done that, since you first came back
from Charleston, and found me alone in New York.
    MRS. H. I found a dear, sweet little daughter. (*Stroking her
head.*) Heaven sent you, darling! You have been a blessing to
me. I hardly know how I should have got through the past few
months at all without you at my side.
    EDITH. What is your own trouble, dear? I have found you
in tears so often; and since last October, after the battle of

Cedar Creek, you—you have never shown me a letter from—from my—Frank's father. General Haverill arrived in Washington yesterday, but has not been here yet. Is it because I am here? He has never seen me, and I feel that he never has forgiven Frank for marrying me.

Mrs. H. Nonsense, my child; he did think the marriage was imprudent, but he told me to do everything I could for you. If General Haverill has not been to see either of us, since his arrival in Washington, it is nothing that you need to worry your dear little head about. How are you getting on with your son's wardrobe?

Edit . Oh! Splendidly! Frankie isn't a baby any longer; he's a man, now, and he has to have a man's clothing! (*Holding up a little pair of trousers, with maternal pride.*) He's rather young to be dressed like a man, but I want Frank to grow up as soon as possible. I long to have him old enough to understand me when I repeat to him the words in which General Haverill told the whole world how his father died! (*Rising.*) And yet, even in his official report to the Government, he only honored him as Lieutenant Bedloe. He has never forgiven his son for the disgrace he brought upon his name.

Mrs. H. I know him so well—(*Rising.*)—the unyielding pride, that conquers even the deep tenderness of his nature. He can be silent, though his own heart is breaking. (*Aside.*) He can be silent, too, though *my* heart is breaking. (*Dropping her face in her hand.*)

Edith. Mother! (*Putting her arm about her.*)

[*Enter* Jannette, l. c.]

Jan. A letter for you, Madam.

Mrs. H. (*Taking note. Aside.*) He has answered me. (*Opens and reads; inclines her head to* Jannette, *who goes out*, l. c., *to hall. Aloud.*) General Haverill will be here this afternoon, Edith. [*Exit* l. c., *and up the stairs.*

Edith. There is something that she cannot confide to me, or to anyone. General Haverill returned to Washington yesterday, and he has not been here yet. He will be here to day. I always tremble when I think of meeting him.

[General Buckthorn *appears in hall*, l. c.]

Buck. Come right in; this way, Barket. Ah, Edith!

Barket. (*Entering*, l. c.) As I was saying, sur—just after the battle of Sayder Creek began (l. c.)——

Buck. (*To* Edith.) More good news! The war is, indeed, over, now!

Barket. Whin Colonel Wist rode to the front to mate his raytrating rigiment——

Buck. General Johnston has surrended his army, also; and that, of course, does end the war.

Edith. I'm very glad that all the fighting is over.

Buck. So am I; but my occupation, and old Barket's, too, is gone. Always at work on new clothes for our little soldier?

Edith. He's growing so, I can hardly make them fast

enough for him. But this is the time for his afternoon nap. I
must go now, to see if he is sleeping soundly.

BUCK. Our dear little mother ! (*Tapping her chin.*) I always
claim the privilege of my white hair, you know. (*She puts up
her lips; he kisses her. She goes out,* R.) The sweetest young
widow I ever saw ! (BARKET *coughs.* BUCK *turns sharply;*
BARKET *salutes.*) Well! What the devil are you thinking about
now ?

BARKET. (C.) The ould time, sur. Yer honor used to claim
the same privilege for brown hair.

BUCK. (C.) You old rascal ! What a memory you have !
You were telling me for the hundredth time about the battle of
Cedar Creek; go on. I can never hear it often enough. Ker-
chival West was a favorite of mine, poor fellow !

BARKET. Just afther the battle of Sayder Creek began, when
the Colonel rode to the front to mate his raytrating rigiment——

BUCK. I'll tell Old Margery to bring in tea for both of us,
Barket.

BARKET. For both of us, sur ?

BUCK. Yes ; and later in the evening we'll have something
else, together. This is a great day for all of us. I'm not your
commander to-day, but your old comrade in arms—(*Laying his
arm over* BARKET's *shoulder.*)—and I'm glad I don't have to pull
myself up now every time I forget my dignity. Ah! you and I
will be laid away before long, but we'll be together again in the
next world, won't we, Barket ?

BARKET. Wid yer honor's permission. (*Saluting.*)

BUCK. Ha—ha—ha! (*Laughing.*) If we do meet there, I'm
certain you'll salute me as your superior officer. There's old
Margery, now. (*Looking* L. *to door. Calls.*) Margery! Tea for
two!

MARGERY. (*Without,* R.) The tay be waiting for ye, sur ; and
it be boilin' over wid impatience.

BUCK. Bring up a chair, Barket. (*Sitting in arm-chair,* C.)

BARKET. (*Having placed table and drawing up a chair.*) Do
you know, Gineral, I don't fale quite aisy in my moind. I'm
not quite sure that Margery will let us take our tay together.
(*Sits down, doubtfully.*)

BUCK. I hadn't thought of that. I—(*Glancing* R.)—I hope she
will, Barket. But, of course, if she won't—she's been com-
mander-in-chief of my household ever since Jenny was a baby.

BARKET. At Fort Duncan, in Texas.

BUCK. You and Old Margery never got along very well in
those days ; but I thought you had made it all up ; she nursed
you through your wound, last summer, and after the battle of
Cedar Creek, also.

BARKET. Yis, sur, bliss her kind heart, she's been like a wife
to me ; and that's the trouble. A man's wife is such an angel
when he's ill that he dreads to get well ; good health is a misfortune to him. Auld Margery and I have had anither misundershtanding.

BUCK. I'll do the best I can for both of us, Barket. You were telling me about the battle of——

BARKET. Just afther the battle of Sayder Creek began, whin Colonel Wist rode to the front to mate his raytrating rigiment—— (*Enter* OLD MARGERY, R., *tray, tea, &c. She stops abruptly,* R. C., *looking at* BARKET. *He squirms in his chair.* BUCKTHORN *rises and stands with his back to the mantel.* OLD MARGERY *moves to the table, arranges things on it, glances at* BAR., *then at* BUCK., *who looks up at ceiling, rubbing his chin, &c.* OLD MARGERY *takes up one of the cups, with saucer.*)

OLD MARG. I misunderstood yer order, sur. I see there's no one here but yerself. (*Going* R.)

BUCK. Ah, Margery! (*She stops,* R. C.) Barket tells me that there has been a slight misunderstanding between you and him.

OLD MARG Day before yisterday, the ould Hibernian dhrone had the kitchen upside down, to show anither ould milithary vagabone loike himself how the battle of Sayder Creek was fought. He knocked the crame pitcher into the basket of clane clothes, and overturned some raspberry jam and the flat-irons into a pan of fresh eggs. There *has* been a misundershtanding betwane us.

BUCK. I see there has. I suppose Barket was showing his friend how Colonel Kerchival West rode forward to meet his regiment, when he was already wounded dangerously.

OLD MARG. Bliss the poor, dear young man! He and I was always good frinds, though he was somethin' of a devil in the kitchen himself, whin he got there. (*Wiping her eye with one corner of her apron.*) And bliss the young Southern lady that was in love wid him, too. (*Changing the cup and wiping the other eye with the corner of her apron.*) Nothing was iver heard of ayther of thim afther that battle was over, to this very day.

BUCK. Barket was at Kerchival's side when he rode to the front. (OLD MARGERY *hesitates a moment, then moves to the table, sets down the cup and marches out,* R. BUCK, *sits in the arm-chair again, pouring tea.*) I could always find some way to get Old Margery to do what I wanted her to do.

BARKET. You're a great man, Ginerel; we'd niver have conquered the South widout such men.

BUCK. Now go on, Barket; you were interrupted.

BARKET. Just afther the battle of Sayder Creek began, whin——

[*Enter* JANNETTE, L. C., *with card, which she hands to* BUCK.]

BUCK. (*Reading card.*) Robert Ellingham! (*Rises.*) I will go to him. (*To* JAN.) You go upstairs and tell Madeline to come down.

JANNETTE. Yes, sir. (*Going.*)

BUCK. And, Jannette, simply say there is a caller; don't tell her who is here. (*Exit* JAN., L. C. *and upstairs.* BUCK. *follows her out to hall.*) Ellingham! My dear fellow! (*Extending his hand and disappearing,* L.)

BARKET. Colonel Ellingham and Miss Madeline—lovers! That's the kind o' volunteers the country nades now!

[*Enter* BUCKTHORN *and* ELLINGHAM, L. C.]

BUCK. (*As he enters.*) We've been fighting four years to keep
you out of Washington, Colonel, but we are delighted to see you
within the lines, now.

ELLING. I am glad, indeed, General, to have so warm a welcome. But can you tell me anything about my sister, Gertrude?

BUCK. About your sister? Why, can't you tell us? And have
you heard nothing of Kerchival West on your side of the line?

ELLING. All I can tell you is this: As soon as possible after
our surrender at Appomatox, I made my way to the Shenandoah
Valley. Our home there is utterly deserted. I have hurried
down to Washington in the hopes that I might learn something of
you. There is no human being about the old homstead; it is like
a haunted house—empty, and dark, and solitary. You do not
even know where Gertrude is?

BUCK. We only know that Kerchival was not found among the
dead of his own regiment at Cedar Creek, though he fell among
them during the fight. The three girls searched the field for him,
but he was not there. As darkness came on, and they were returning to the house, Gertrude suddenly seized the bridle of a
stray horse, sprang upon its back and rode away to the South,
into the woods at the foot of Three Top Mountain. The other two
girls watched for her in vain. She did not return, and we have
heard nothing from her since.

ELLING. Poor girl! I understand what was in her thoughts,
and she was right. We captured fourteen hundred prisoners that
day, although we were defeated, and Kerchival must have been
among them. Gertrude rode away, alone, in the darkness, to find
him. I shall return to the South at once and learn where she now
is.

[JANNETTE *has entered, down the stairs*, L. C.]

JANNETTE. Miss Madeline will be down in a moment.
[*Exit in hall,* L.

BARKET. (*Aside,* up C.) That name wint through his chist like
a rifle ball.

BUCK. Will you step into the drawing-room, Colonel? I will
see Madeline myself, first. She does not even know that you are
living.

ELLING. I hardly dared ask for her. (*Passing; turns.*) Is
she well?

BUCK. Yes; and happy—or soon will be.

ELLING. Peace, at last! (*Exit,* L. 2 E., *to apartment.* BUCK.
closes portieres)

BUCK. I ought to prepare Madeline a little, Barket; you must
help me.

BARKET. Yis, sur, I will.

[*Enter* MADELINE, L. C., *down the stairs.*]

MADELINE. Uncle! Jannette said you wished to see me;
there is a visitor here. Who is it?

BARKET. Colonel Robert Ellingham.

MAD. Ah! (*Staggering.*)

BUCK. (*Supporting her.*) You infernal idiot! I'll put you in the guard-house!

BARKET. You wanted me to help ye, Gineral.

MAD. Robert is alive—and here? (*Rising from his arms, she moves to the portieres, holds them aside, peeping in; gives a joyful start, tosses aside the portieres and runs through.*)

BUCK. Barket! There's nothing but that curtain between us and Heaven.

BARKET. I don't fale like stayin' out o' Hiven, mysilf, sur. Gineral! I'll kiss Ould Margery—if I die for it! [*Exit* R.

BUCK. Kiss Old Margery! I'll give him a soldier's funeral. (*Walking* R. *Enter* JENNY, L. C., *from hall*, L. C., *demurely.*) Ah! Jenny, my dear! I have news for you. Colonel Robert Ellingham is in the drawing-room.

JENNY. Oh! I am delighted. (*Starting* L.)

BUCK. A-h-e-m!

JEN. Oh!—exactly. I see. I have some news for you, papa. Captain Heartsease has arrived in Washington.

BUCK. Oh! My dear! I have often confessed to you how utterly mistaken I was about that young man. He is a soldier —as good a soldier as you are. I'll ask him to the house.

JEN. (*Demurely.*) He is here now.

BUCK. Now?

JEN. He's been here an hour; in the library.

BUCK. Why! Barket and I were in the library fifteen minutes ago.

JEN. Yes, sir. We were in the bay-window; the curtains were closed.

BUCK. Oh! exactly; I see. You may tell him he has my full consent.

JEN. He hasn't asked for it.

BUCK. Hasn't he? And you've been in the bay-window an hour? Well, my darling—I was considered one of the best Indian fighters in the old army, but it took me four years to propose to your mother. I'll go and see the Captain. [*Exit*, L. C., *to hall*, L.

JEN. I wonder if it will take Captain Heartsease four years to propose to me. Before he left Washington, nearly two years ago, he told everybody in the circle of my acquaintance, except me, that he was in love with me. I'll be an old lady in caps before our engagement commences. Poor, dear mother! The idea of a girl's waiting four years for a chance to say, "Yes." It's been on the tip of my tongue so often, I'm afraid it'll pop out, at last, before he pops the question.

[*Enter* BUCK. *and* HEARTSEASE, L. C., *from hall.*]

BUCK. Walk right in, Captain; this is the family room. You must make yourself quite at home here.

HEARTSEASE. Thank you. (*Walking down* R.)

BUCK. My dear! (*Apart to Jenny.*) The very first thing he said to me, after our greeting, was that he loved my daughter.

JEN. Now he's told my father!

BUCK. He's on fire!

JEN. Is he? (*Looking at* HEARTSEASE, *who stands quietly,* R., *stroking his mustache.*) Why doesn't he tell *me?*

BUCK. You may have to help him a little; your mother assisted me. (*Turning up* C.) When you and Jenny finish your chat, Captain—(*Lighting a cigar at the mantel.*)—you must join me in the smoking room.

HEART. I shall be delighted. By the way, General—I have been in such a fever of excitement since I arrived at this house——

JEN. (*Aside.*) Fever? Chills!

HEART. That I forgot it entirely. I have omitted a very important and a very sad commission. I have brought with me the note-book of Lieutenant Frank Bedloe—otherwise Haverill—in which Miss Gertrude Ellingham wrote down his last message to his young wife.

JEN. Have you seen Gertrude?

BUCK. (*Taking book.*) How did this note-book come into your possession?

HEART. Miss Ellingham visited the prison in North Carolina where I was detained. She was going from hospital to hospital, from prison to prison, and from burial-place to burial-place, to find Colonel Kerchival West, if living—or some record of his death.

BUCK. Another Evangeline! Searching for her lover through the wilderness of this great war !

HEART. I was about to be exchanged at the time, and she requested me to bring this to her friends in Washington. She had not intended to carry it away with her. I was not exchanged, as we then expected, but I afterwards escaped from prison to General Sherman's Army.

BUCK. I will carry this long-delayed message to the widowed young mother.   [*Exit* R.

JEN. I remember so well, when poor Lieutenant Haverill took out the note-book and asked Gertrude to write for him. He —he brought me a message at the same time. (*Their eyes meet. He puts up his glasses. She turns away, touching her eyes.*)

HEART. I—I remember the circumstances you probably allude to; that is—when he left my side—I—I gave him my—I mean your—lace handkerchief.

JEN. It is sacred to me!

HEART. Y-e-s—I would say—is it?

JEN. (*Wiping her eyes.*) It was stained with the life-blood of a hero!

HEART. I must apologize to you for it's condition. I hadn't any chance to have it washed and ironed.

JEN. (*Looking around at him, suddenly; then, aside.*) What could any girl do with a lover like that? (*Turning up stage.*)

HEART. (*Aside.*) She seems to remember that incident so tenderly! My blood boils!

JEN. Didn't you long to see you—your friends at home—when you were in prison, Captain?

HEART. Yes—especially—I longed especially, Miss Buckthorn, to see——

JEN. Yes—to see——

HEART. But there were lots of jolly fellows in the prison. (JENNY *turns away.*)

HEART. We had a dramatic society, and a glee club, and an orchestra. I was one of the orchestra. I had a banjo with one string; I played one tune on it, that I used to play on the piano, with one finger. But, Miss Buckthorn, I am a prisoner again, to-night—your prisoner.

JEN. (*Aside.*) At last !

HEART. I'll show you how that tune went. (*Turns to piano; sits.*)

JEN. (*Aside.*) Papa said I'd have to help him, but I don't see an opening. (*Heartsease plays part of an air with one finger; strikes two or three wrong notes.*)

HEART. There are two notes down there, somewhere, that I never could get right. The fellows in prison used to dance while I played—(*Playing.*)—that is, the lame ones did ; those that wern't lame couldn't keep the time.

JEN. You must have been in great danger, Captain, when you escaped from prison.

HEART. Y-e-s. I was badly frightened several times. One night I came face to face, on the road, with a Confederate Officer. It was Captain Thornton.

JEN. Oh! What did you do?

HEART. I killed him. (*Very quietly, and trying the tune again at once. Enter* JANNETTE, *from* L., *in hall; she glances into the room and goes up the stairs.*) I used to skip those two notes on the banjo. It's very nice for a soldier to come home from the war, and meet those—I mean the one particular person—that he—you see, when a soldier loves a woman, as—as——

JEN. (*Aside.*) As he loves me. (*Approaches him.*)

HEART. As soldiers often do—(*Plays; she turns away, petulantly; he plays the tune through correctly.*) That's it !

JEN. (*Aside.*) I'm not going to be made love to by piece-meal, like this, any longer. (*Aloud.*) Captain Heartsease! Have you anything in particular to say to me ? (*He looks up.*)

HEART. Y-e-s. (*Rising.*)

JEN. Say it! You told my father, and all my friends, that you were in love with me. Whom are you going to tell next?

HEART. I *am* in love with you.

JEN. It was my turn.

HEART. (*Going near to her.*) Do you love me?

JEN. (*Laying her head quietly on his breast.*) I must take time to consider.

HEART. (*Quietly.*) I assume that this means " Yes."

JEN. It isn't the way a girl says " No."

HEART. My darling !

JEN. Why ! His heart is beating as fast as mine is !

HEART. (*Quietly.*) I am frantic with joy. (*He kisses her. She hides her face on his breast. Enter* MRS. HAVERILL, L. C., *down-stairs, followed by* JANNETTE. MRS. HAVERILL *stops suddenly, up* L. C. JANNETTE *stands in the doorway.* HEARTSEASE *inclines his head to her, quietly looking at her over* JENNY.) I am delighted to see you, after so long an absence; I trust that we shall meet more frequently hereafter.

JEN. (*Looking at him.*) Eh?

HEART. (*Looking down at her.*) I think, perhaps, it might be as well for us to repair to another apartment, and continue our interview, there!

JEN. (*Dropping her head on his breast again.*) This room is very comfortable.

MRS. H. Jenny, dear! (JENNY *starts up; looks from* MRS. H. *to* HEART.)

JEN. Constance! I—'Bout face! March! (*Turns and goes out,* R.)

MRS. H. I am glad to see you again, Captain, and happy as well as safe.

HEART. Than you, Madam, I am happy. If you will excuse me, I will join—my father—in the smoking-room. (MRS. H. *inclines her head, and* HEART. *walks out,* R.)

MRS. H. Jannette! You may ask General Haverill to come into this room. (*Exit* JAN., L. MRS. H. *walks down* R., *reading a note.*) "I have hesitated to come to you personally, as I have hesitated to write to you. If I have been silent, it is because I could not bring my hand to write what was in my mind and in my heart. I do not know that I can trust my tongue to speak it, but I will come."

[*Enter* HAVERILL, L. C., *from hall; he stops, up* L. C.]

HAVER. Constance!

MRS. H. My husband! May I call you husband? After all these months of separation, with your life in almost daily peril, and my life—what? Only a weary longing for one loving word—and you are silent.

HAVER. May I call you wife? I do not wish to speak that word except with reverence. You have asked me to come to you. I am here. I will be plain, direct and brief. Where is the portrait of yourself, which I gave you, in Charleston, for my son?

MRS. H. Your son is dead, sir; and my portrait lies upon his breast, in the grave. (HAVER. *takes the miniature from his pocket and holds it towards her in his extended hand. She starts back.*) He gave it to you? And you ask me where it is?

HAVER. It might have lain in the grave of Kerchival West!

MRS. H. Ah!

HAVER. Not in my son's. I found it upon *his* breast. (*She turns front, dazed.*) Well! I am listening! It was not I that sought this interview, madam; and if you prefer to remain silent, I will go. You know, now, why I have been silent so long.

MRS. H. My only witnesses to the truth are both dead. I shall remain silent. (*Turning towards him.*) We stand before each other, living, but not so happy as they. We are parted, forever. Even if you should accept my unsupported word—if I could so far forget my pride as to give it to you—suspicion would still hang between us. I remain silent. (HAVERILL *looks at her, earnestly, for a moment, then approaches her.*)

HAVER. I cannot look into your eyes and not see truth and loyalty there. Constance!

MRS. H. No, John! (*Checking him.*) I will not accept your blind faith! (*Moving, L.*)

HAVER. (*Looking down at the picture in his hand.*) My faith is blind; blind as my love! I do not wish to see! (*Enter* EDITH. R. *She stops; looks at* HAVERILL. *He raises his head and looks at her.*)

EDITH. This is General Haverill? (*Dropping her eyes.*) I am Edith, sir.

HAVER. (*Gently.*) My son's wife. (*Kisses her forehead.*) You shall take the place he once filled in my heart. His crime and his disgrace are buried in a distant grave.

EDITH. And you have not forgiven him, even yet?

MRS H. Is there no atonement for poor Frank's sin—not even his death? Can you only bury the wrong and forget the good?

HAVER. The good?

MRS. H. Your own words to the Government, as his commander!

HAVER. What do you mean?

MRS. H. "The victory of Cedar Creek would have been impossible without the sacrifice of this young Officer."

HAVER. My own words, yes—but——

EDITH. "His name must take its place, forever, in the roll of names which his countrymen honor."

HAVER. Lieutenant Bedloe!

MRS. H. Haverill! You did not know?

HAVER. My—son!

EDITH. You did not receive mother's letter?—after his death?

HAVER. My son! (*Sinking upon chair or ottoman.*) I left him alone in his grave, unknown; but my tears fell for him then, as they do now. He died before I reached him.

EDITH. Father! (*Laying her hand gently on his shoulder.*) You shall see Frank's face again. His little son is lying asleep upstairs; and when he wakes up, Frank's own eyes will look into yours.

HAVER. My daughter!

EDITH. I have just received his last message. I will read it to you. (*Note-book. Reads.*) "Tell our little son how his father died, not how he lived. And tell her who filled my own mother's place so lovingly." (*She looks at* MRS. HAVERILL, *moves to her and hides her face in her bosom.*) My mother!

MRS. H. Edith—my child! Frank loved us both.

EDITH. (*Reading.*) "Father's portrait of her, which she gave to me in Charleston—(*Haverill starts.*)—helped me to be a better man."

HAVER. (*Rising to his feet.*) Constance!

EDITH. (*Reading.*) "It was taken from me in Richmond, and it is in the possession of Captain Edward Thornton."

HAVER. One moment! Stop! Let me think! (EDITH *looks at him; retires up* L. C.) Thornton was a prisoner—and to Kerchival West. A despatch had been found upon him—he was searched! (*He moves to her and takes both her hands in his own, bowing his head over them.*) My head is bowed in shame.

MRS. H. Speak to me, John, as you used to speak! Tell me you still love me!

HAVER. The—the words will come—but they are—choking me —now. (*Presses her hand to his lips.*)

MRS. H. We will think no more of the past, except of what was bright in it. Frank's memory, and our own love, will be with us always.

[*Enter* BUCKTHORN, R., *followed by* HEARTSEASE.]

BUCK. Haverill! You are back from the war, too. It begins to look like peace in earnest.

HAVER. Yes. Peace and home. (*Shaking hands with him,* C. MRS. H. *joins* EDITH.)

[*Enter* BARKET, R.]

BARKET. Gineral! (BUCK. *moves to him.* HAVER. *joins* MRS. H. *and* EDITH. BARKET *speaks apart, twisting one side of his face.*) I kissed her!

BUCK. Have you sent for a surgeon?

BARKET. I felt as if the inimy had surprised us agin, and Sheridan was sixty miles away.

HAVER. This is old Sergeant Barket. (BAR. *salutes.*) You were the last man of us all that saw Colonel West.

BARKET. Just afther the battle of Sayder Creek began— whin Colonel Wist rode to the front to mate his retrating rigiment—the byes formed in line, at sight of him, to raysist the victorious inimy. It was just at the brow of a hill—about there, sur—(*Pointing with his cane.*) and—here!—(*He takes tray from table and sets it on the carpet, down* R. C. *Lays the slices of bread in a row.*) That be the rigiment (*All interested.* MADELINE and ELLINGHAM *enter,* L , *and look on.* BARKET *arranges the two cups and saucers in a row.*) That be the inimy's batthery, sur. (*Enter* MARGERY, R. *She goes to the table, then looks around, sharply, at* BARKET.)

OLD MARG. Ye ould Hibernian dhrone! What are yez doin' wid the china on the floor? You'll break it all!

BUCK. Ah—Margery! Barket is telling us where he last saw Colonel Kerchival West.

OLD MARG. The young Colonel! The tay-cups and saucers be's the inimy's batthery? Yez may smash 'em, if ye lolke!

BUCK. Go on, BARKET. (JEN. and HEARTSEASE *have entered; as* BAR. *proceeds, the whole party lean forward, intensely interested.* GERT. *enters in hall, looks in, beckons out* L. KERCHIVAL *follows. They move to* C., *up stage, back of the rest and unseen, listening.*)

BARKET. Just as the rigiment was rayformed in line, and Colonel Wist was out in front—widout any coat or hat, and wid

ҁ y a shtick in his hand—we heard cheers in the rear. Gineral
eridan was coming! One word to the men—and we swept
. ɪr the batthery like a whirlwind! (*Slashing his cane through
cups and saucers.*)

'LD MARG. Hoo—roo!

BARKET. The attack on the lift plank was checked. But when
shtopped to take breath, Colonel Wist wasn't wid us. (GERT.
· ɴs *lovingly to* KERCHIVAL. *He places his arm about her.*)
aven knows where he is now. Afther the battle was over, poor
ɴs Gertrude wint off by hersilf into the wilderness to find him.

ҁER. My wife! You saved my life, at last! (*Embracing her.*)

BARKET. They'll niver come together agin in this world. I
v Miss Gertrude, myself, ride away into the woods and disap-
ɪr behind a school-house on the battle-field, over there.

ɢERT. No, Barket—(*All start and look.*)—it was the little
urch; we were married there this morning!

CURTAIN.